TA... OF
OLD...

James Berry

Edited by Gertrude M. Horgan

ROBINSON PUBLISHING

with

Published in association with
The Dolmen Press

ROBINSON PUBLISHING
with Breslich & Foss
11 Shepherd House
5 Shepherd Street
London W1Y 7LD

Published in association with The Dolmen Press

First published by The Dolmen Press 1966
as *Tales of the West of Ireland*
Published by Robinson Publishing 1984
© Gertrude M. Horgan
Series design: Lawrence & Gerry Design Group

ISBN 1 85004 022 2

Printed in Great Britain by
Richard Clay (The Chaucer Press) Ltd
Bungay
Suffolk

FOREWORD

James Berry, the author of these tales was a farmer by vocation and a narrator of traditional tales by avocation. He was born in Bunowen, near Louisburgh, County Mayo, in 1842, and a number of his early recollections are centred around the persons and events of the Great Famine. His parents were John Berry and Bridget O'Malley. References to the O'Malley clan and to the Western Owls of the O'Malleys predominate in the tales which in his old age he recalled from oral narration for publication in *The Mayo News* for the benefit of posterity in the years 1910–1913.

Berry's education was received in the hedge schools of his native region and was supplemented by the guidance given to his later reading by his uncle, Father Ned O'Malley, Parish Priest of Carna in Connemara. In his youth, James Berry used to visit his uncle, and it was in Carna that he met Sarah Greene, the young Connemara girl who was later to become his wife. After his marriage he settled in Carna where he reared his family, toiled as a farmer to support them, and persevered in his lifelong devotion to the art of storytelling. In 1914 he was buried in Mynish cemetery where he now rests beside the bodies of his wife and his mother.

His daughter, Miss Helena Berry, who still lives in Carna, recalls that her father spent many hours at night by the fire recording the traditional tales in numerous notebooks. She remembers that when he was dying, he called his wife to his side and made her burn a heap of ledgers which contained the stories he was still preparing for publication, saying that he did not wish anyone else to tamper with the narratives.

The folk tales which James Berry recorded and in some cases invented do not possess the range and imaginative quality of William Carleton's writings, but in many ways the Mayo man's delineation of the faith of the peasants and the devotion of their priests reveals aspects of the life of the Irish people which Carleton, who wrote often for temporal gain and as a paid propagandist, frequently burlesques and derides. D. J. O'Donoghue notes that Carleton was prepared to write for any and every side provided he received payment. By contrast, James Berry wrote tales out of love for his people and his country.

In arranging the tales in this volume, I have endeavoured to remain true to the art of Irish story-tradition and to the spirit of James Berry. The editing process throughout has been controlled by a desire to modernize the presentation of the material so that a number of short tales which were previously combined in lengthy summaries of incidents have been separated and given their just due. The division of the work into Tales of Mayo and Tales of Connemara is my designation, not Berry's, and the titles of a number of the tales are the responsibility of the editor. All things considered, this collection of tales is offered "To James Berry and the people of Ireland with love!"

G.M.H.

ACKNOWLEDGMENTS

While studying Anglo-Irish literature in Ireland in 1964–1965, I spent several months at a cottage owned by Mr. and Mrs. P. J. Kelly of Westport, and located at Old Head, on the shore of Clew Bay, a short distance from Croagh Patrick. Through conversations with the Kellys I became interested in the work of James Berry, their favourite Irish author, a native of Bunowen near Louisburgh in County Mayo. At the time I was engaged in research on the career and accomplishments of William Carleton, the best known teller of Irish tales in the nineteenth century. Carleton's tales were at least available, although no recent editions have been published with the exception of a small collection edited by Anthony Cronin.

In the case of James Berry, I found that his tales had been published in *The Mayo News*, and since the files of this newspaper for the years in question had been destroyed, the only available copies were those which had been saved by Mayo residents, or were in the files of the periodical collection of the British Museum. A heritage which belongs to the people of Ireland, a number of traditional tales of Mayo and Connemara, was on the verge of being forgotten unless these stories could be collected and edited in permanent form. This was the task to which I dedicated myself in gratitude to my Irish ancestors, the Horgans of County Cork, the Coynes of Athlone, an the O'Neills and Donahues of County Tyrone.

To Mr. and Mrs. P. J. Kelly, their son, Father Vincent Kelly, and their daughter Breta I am indebted for the preservation of a number of the Berry tales, and for their warm-hearted enthusiasm and encouragement. Mr. Seamus Durkan of Louisburgh devoted many hours to accompanying me on drives throughout the area to the townlands mentioned in these tales. He also introduced me to Mr. Austin O'Reilly, the local historian, who knew James Berry, and who is himself a repository of memories and stories which deserve preservation. A visit to Carna in County Galway led to an interview with Miss Helena Berry, daughter of James, who was happy to grant permission for this edition of her father's tales. Father Leo Morahan, a native of Louisburgh, now teaching at St. Mary's College, Galway, and also serving as editor of *An Coinneal*, a magazine published by Kilgeever Parish, Louisburgh, was most helpful in locating some of the missing tales at the British Museum.

Mr. Liam Miller of The Dolmen Press, to whom I was introduced through the kindness of Mr. William O'Neill of Trumera National School, Mountrath, County Lapis, evinced interest in publishing these tales of the West of Ireland as part of a series on Ireland's cultural past. He has been helpful in his suggestions and patient in the necessary delays encountered in preparing the manuscript. The administration of Aquinas College, Grand Rapids, Michigan, where I am a member of the faculty in the Department of English Literature, generously granted me the time and assistance required for the compilation of this volume.

Gertrude M. Horgan

Old Head, County Mayo, July-September, 1964
Dublin, October, 1964–January, 1965
Nantasket Beach, Hull, Massachusetts, August, 1965.

PART ONE

TALES OF MAYO

A PARLIAMENTARY ELECTION DURING THE FAMINE

About the year 1848, although the famine was raging and denuding the country of its inhabitants by the thousands each day, a Parliamentary election took place in Mayo which roused the peasantry to a great pitch, and was contested on both sides with extraordinary virulence and determination. One of the candidates was G. H. Moore of Moorehall, the nominee of the Brownes of Westport, for Moore was their near kinsman, an untried man at that time, and the electors of West Mayo distrusted him in consequence of having some of the blood of the notorious Brownes in his veins. One of the reasons for their distrust was a terrible tradition perpetuated by the old men of the West who always said that Denis Browne, the tyrant, was nicknamed "Soap the Rope" because of all the people he got hanged in 1798 as well as before and after that date. It was said that Browne was responsible for having G. H. Moore's grandfather hanged for some crime, and yet the degenerate son of the man who was slaughtered forgot all about this and married either the daughter or the niece of Denis Browne. I don't know whether this terrible story was true or false, but I do know that I have heard it a thousand times from my infancy until I grew to be a man, and the old men who used to be telling the tale knew what they were talking about, for they knew the Moores who owned one townland in the parish of Louisburgh, namely Aillemore, some four miles west of the town. The Moores were not considered kind landlords either, for their tenants scarcely saw any of their faces, but were left to the mercy of the grasping bailiff.

I

The other candidate in this election marched beneath the banner of the "Lion of the fold of Judah," the great John McHale of Tuam, the great, stalwart, militant prelate with the pale face and the massive Roman nose, who could well be called "Gregory the Great of Ireland." Oh, it's often and often I when young and thousands with me, went to meet him all the way towards Lecanvey, carrying evergreen branches high above our heads, and when he would draw near our joyous shouts would rend the air and Croagh Patrick would echo with our cries, for to us he seemed like Conn of the hundred battles triumphantly returning from the wars.

If the Archbishop searched all Ireland he couldn't have found a worse candidate than his nominee, Joe Moore McDonnell of Doocastle, a country squire, who had nothing to recommend him save his drinking proclivities, his vile, immoral, immodest anecdotes, and his colossal stature; but the great Archbishop could find no other candidate, and he was determined to oust Moore at any cost in order to show the Government and the landlords what he could do. Some thought it a rash, forlorn hope, but the Archbishop was undismayed for, like the first Napoleon, he had a staff of priests around him, generals in fact, who were the bravest of the brave, foremost among them being Father Peter Conway, Father Luke Ryan, and Father Michael Curley who, although small in stature, was surely the Roman of them all.

The list of voters in my native parish was much reduced, for the small freeholders were swept away in hundreds by the famine and were mouldering in their grave, and those who remained and withstood its ravages were impudent boddagha who always plumped for the

Brownes, so the case seemed dark and hopeless in the West. However, the night before the polling day came around, the then Parish Priest of Louisburgh, Father Par McManus, gathered all the young men of that town and adjacent villages around him and held a consultation. They disguised themselves and became kidnappers, and they went through the whole parish in gangs and lifted everyone of Browne's plumpers off their beds, abducted and carried them to the P.P's house where they remained strictly guarded until the news arrived that Joe Moore McDonnell was returned M.P. for Mayo.

The first man they took off his bed was the old packman Pat Malley of Shraugh, who at all times worked tooth and nail for the Brownes of Westport. When seized, Pat began lustily calling for his sons who were great fighting men to come and rescue him. "Joe Malley," he shouted, "where are you? Johnny, Affy, Myles, come here at once with your blackthorns!" But they didn't respond to his call for it was his own sons and others who kidnapped him. They carried him through the fields and had to jump across a sluggish stream called the Glesh before they placed him in Father McManus's parlour. All through this journey the old man kept threatening his abductors that "as sure as there is a Browne, or a Clendinning or a Hildebrand in Westport ye will pay dearly for this!" The kidnappers were inexorable, however, and they secured him under lock and key.

Just then another gang arrived carrying in old Paddy McGirr, Michael McHale and Michael McDonnell, and soon two or three other gangs arrived carrying old Billy na Mallagh of Glankeen, old Wat Malley of Furmoyle, old Johnny Davy Gibbons of Cloonlara, and old Paddy

3

Gibbons of Roonith, the last-named being Lord Sligo's bailiff in the West, and many others of lesser note too numerous to mention. This wasn't a bad night's work for the kidnappers; they surely gave good value for the whiskey they were drinking, and they well deserved it. This business cost the priest some money, for the kidnappers could drink whiskey with the gusto of red men, and the abducted plumpers could drink punch by the gallon; they could throw it back and it wouldn't affect them any more than if you were throwing it into a limekiln in full blast. When the old plumpers saw how the game was played and saw plenty of punch on the table, they threw in the sponge and became very good-humoured, and then they set to work hammer and tongs at the punch, and as the night wore on old McGirr proposed that the old pack-man would spin them a yarn to pass the time away.

PAT MALLEY'S TALE OF THE FACTION FIGHTS OF THE GALVANAGHS AND GROMASTOONS

"Paddy," said old McGirr, "tell us about the faction fights of the Galvanaghs and the Gromastoons, and what was the origin of those curious names." Pat Malley, the old packman, was in the midst of finishing his twelfth tumbler of punch, so he finished it up with a smack before he replied with a smile, "Oh yes, Mr. McGirr, I shall with pleasure, but in doing so I will have to call Irish history to aid me, for I must go into detail which may seem to you to be out of place, but when I have finished you will plainly see what I have been driving at all the time, nor can I explain the thing to the satisfaction of the company without doing so.

"When the Anglo-Normans came over to Ireland with Strongbow, there was a man named De Exter among them, and as time went on some of his descendants grasped a large territory around Swinford and Straide in this county of ours, and they called themselves Jordans. Later on, Cromwell came along and drove out the Anglo-Normans, but in many cases Cromwell gave them a sort of equivalent holding in the wilds of Connacht. Anyone who reads Prendergast's *Cromwellian Settlement* can see this for himself. The ones that Cromwell drove out could take their tenants who wished to follow them into exile. So Cromwell drove out the Jordans of Rosslavin, or one of them, and he gave that Jordan a little patch as an equivalent in the Western Owl of the O'Malley's, namely Old Head, Legan, Balure, Derrylahan, Ruan and Caraclaggin. All these townlands save Caraclaggin are now wiped off the map of Ireland and are encompassed by a double stone wall, and they go by the name of Wilbraham's farm.

"Jordan had to migrate, and he built his humble home in Legan on the bright, sunny, western slope of the hill of Old Head, which commanded a fine view of the valley of the great Achill mountains, Clare Island, and the wild, western Atlantic, and there his descendants dwelt for ages. Four of his tenants, most respectable people, determined to accompany him into exile to share his joys and his sorrows with him in the land of the stranger. One family was named McHale, the ancestor of the McHales of Emlagh; another family was named Durkan, the ancestor of the Durkans of Caraclaggin, some of whom now reside in Askalaun. A third family was named McNicholas, the

5

ancestors of the Nicholsons of Bunowen, who, when they reached the West, dropped the Mc from their name. As time went on, the children of these migrants intermarried with the children of the fine old stock who dwelt along the shore of the western sea, and in a generation or two they became so amalgamated and merged that they were all called Galvanaghs or Galanaghs, because their ancestors came from the barony of Gallan.

"The last family of the amiable Jordans lived some forty years ago in Ballyhaunis. Until very lately they owned some eight acres of sterile land and a two storey house which was fast beginning to decay, in Kelsallagh. It stood on the brow of the cliff above the wild waves in the bleakest spot I have ever seen. There it stood for ages in its nakedness without a tree or bush to shelter it or wave their stunted branches in the wind, and when I passed it by I always compared it in my mind to an aged peasant whose kith and kin all lay slumbering in their graves, and whose children had deserted him and fled in exile across the dark blue sea, while he was left perishing and lamenting on the wild seashore with none to console or comfort him. This was the last bower of the lost paradise of the Jordans, and they clung to it as if it were a fairy palace standing in the Elysian fields. It was the very last remnant of their patrimony in the West and they clung to it with the tenacious grip of an octopus until the last of them perished and the stock became extinct.

"The Gromastoons took their name from an unpalatable wild potato called gromastoon, and these obscure people were something like the Plebeians of ancient Rome. They lived in Falduff, Kilgeever, Moneen and other villages east and north of Louisburgh. Surely they were a

6

very heterogeneous race who lived in squalid poverty and destitution. Most of them were squatters who had no land save conacre, and so they sowed the potato which grew the largest and most numerous tubers, and that was the gromastoon, so the name stuck to them although they surely detested it, and they detested the Galvanaghs whose status was so far above them. It would take only a small spark to explode a fire and set them at the throats of the people they hated.

"When roused, the Gromastoons were a relentless people who would follow up a quarrel even to the very death. Their capital was Moneen, a sort of town of thatched cabins clustered around the spot where a man named Ody Moran lived some forty years ago, and woe to the benighted traveller who had to pass through it, for what the Bowery and Chinatown are to New York, Moneen was to the people of the West. The Gromastoons were so numerous that they could bring six hundred fighting men to the field of battle, followed always by three hundred of their squaws.

"The cause of the quarrel between the Gromastoons and Galvanaghs arose in this way. Two old men who were brothers-in-law and who had seen better days, opened an Academy in Moneen. They were Galvanaghs; one taught reading and writing, and the other taught arithmetic which was called cyphering in those days. On a certain day one of the venerable professors thrashed a chap named O'Donnell, whose father was nicknamed 'the Rebel', a thorough Gromastoon. Next day 'the Rebel' came and thrashed the two venerable professors within an inch of their lives, and when he had them well-thrashed and was leaving the Academy he said, 'I'd do

7

that to any two Galvanaghs in the parish.' Some days after this O'Donnell was on his way from Balower where he lived to Louisburgh, and he had to pass through Bunowen to get there. A Galvanagh came up to him as he was going by, and said, 'Are you as good a man today as the day you thrashed the two old schoolmasters, Billy Lavelle and Owen O'Malley?' 'I am that, if not even better,' said 'the Rebel.' 'Well now, defend yourself,' said the Galvanagh, who proceeded to give him a terrible thrashing. Then the two clans took sides and the war began, a real war between twelve hundred men, for each party brought six hundred fighting men to the field. They fought on Sundays and holydays, at fairs and patterns, at wakes and funerals, and for years every man carried his life in his hand, and even the military could not put the fighting down.

"For a number of years Louisburgh and the country west of it was in a state of siege, and all communication was cut off from Westport, for the road ran through the enemy's stronghold of Moneen, Kilgeever and Falduff. There was no other road then, for the new road from Kelsallagh to Louisburgh wasn't built in those days, and woe to the Galvanagh who attempted to break through the lines held by the Gromastoons!

"On Christmas Day in the year 1829 when the people were coming out from the noonday Mass, the news spread that the Gromastoons were marching on the town nine hundred strong, and a panic set in, for half to two-thirds of the Galvanaghs had been to the midnight Mass and returned to their homes, for they never imagined that the Gromastoons would attack them on that blessed day of all days in the year. Then scouts were sent out on horseback and on foot calling in the absent Galvanaghs, and the town was in a panic and uproar.

"The prospect looked gloomy for the unprepared Galvanaghs, but like Leonides of old who led his band of hardy veterans to meet the hordes of Persia, Billy Nicholson, the veteran leader of the Galvanaghs, led forth his hardy band, determined to meet the hordes of the enemy and cover himself with glory. He took up a strong position at the end of the street where the road sloped down and the wings of his little band were protected by the houses on both sides.

"The motley hordes drew near, led as usual by Peter Ward, a stone mason of Moneen; they hurled themselves against the Galvanaghs and the battle began. The town re-echoed with the shouts of twelve hundred men engaged in mortal strife, the shrieks of women and the rattle of twelve hundred sticks. The Gromastoons began to fall in hundreds, for now all the absent Galvanaghs had hastened to the aid of their comrades, and as the Gromastoons fell their wives drew them down into a vacant space which soon was piled high with bodies. Nothing was heard that blessed day but the rattle of sticks, the shouting of men and the shrieking of women, and when the shades of night were closing around them the Celtic death wail arose on the gale and was wafted through the town for Jimmy Hoban, a Gromastoon, lay on the street stark dead with scores of women weeping around him with the weird cries of so many banshees.

"The battle was over, and the Gromastoons retired, carrying their wounded with them, most of them maimed and disfigured for life, but the Galvanaghs had scarcely a scratch .Wasn't this a nice kind of work on that blessed

9

day? Of course, there was an inquest held which resulted in the transportation of many for twenty years to Van Diemensland. What they suffered there has been described in the street ballads of those days:

> 'So now we're safely landed upon the Australian shore,
> Where thousands of those negroes surrounded o'er and o'er;
> They tackled us like horses as you may understand,
> And they yoked us to the plough, my boys, to plough Van Diemensland.' "

HOW MAURA-NEE-ORTHA WON THE RACE AT BALLYKNOCK

Pat Malley, the old packman, tossed back a few tumblers of punch while Michael McHale tried to get his attention. Finally Paddy, his thirst satisfied, smiled and looked around him. McHale called across the room to him, "Paddy, how did you come by that mare of yours, Maura-nee-Ortha?"

"I came by her quite accidentally," said Paddy, "and I will tell you about it. When I gave up being a packman and got married, I rented the townland of Shraugh which was wasteland from Lord Sligo and I built my home there, and became a cattle jobber. One day I was going to the fair of Ballyheame or perhaps it was to Doon-na-Mona I was going, I cannot recall which, but I was mounted on a six year old gray mare that was rather slow.

"When I drew near my destination I met an old man who was leading a young bay mare with a straddle and baskets on her. She began to prance about and she threw off the baskets and the straddle turned under her belly as she lashed about in a great way so that she soon got rid of the straddle. Then I saw that she was the most beautiful bright bay mare I had ever seen. The simple old peasant was in a rage.

" 'What's up with you, man?' I said to him. 'Arra man, don't you see what is up with me? Amn't I killed entirely with this rip of a brumach? May the curse of Cromwell fall down on the top iv her head,' he said.

" 'Why did you buy such a wild one?' I said. 'Arra, sure didn't I get grief and misfortune when I got this one'? said he. 'But I didn't buy her, I reared her myself. Some four years ago I had an old bay mare who in her time was surely a good one. I lived near Moorehall, and the Moores were always famous for having great horses. They had at that time a wonderful thoroughbred sire, and I bribed the groom who at night let the sire serve my mare, and this is the vagabond she brought me.'

" 'Would you swap with me?' I said. 'Ah! God forgive you for humbugging an old man,' he said. 'I'll take her as she stands,' I said. 'Well, then, here she is and my blessing,' he replied. I dismounted and took the saddle off my gray mare and placed it on Maura-nee-Ortha's back and drove off, followed by the blessing and prayers of the old man.

"Soon after this they started a horse race in Louisburgh; of course there was no racecourse, only the public road, the distance being from Kilgeever to Louisburgh. There were horses there from Aughagower, Kilmeenan and elsewhere, and off they went, Maura among them. When they were midway between Moneen and Toureen, as Maura was passing swiftly by, the Aughagower man put his foot under the stirrup of Maura's jockey and shot him out of the saddle. The mare halted until the jockey got back in the saddle and before they reached the Bay of Toureen she swept past the lot of them, nor could her jockey pull her up until she reached Bunowen, and when he got her in hand and turned, she danced through the square in such a way that the old men swore in their excitement. 'By G—!' they cried, 'she's ready to run to the Killary Bay!'

"At that time Lord Sligo had a racecourse in a portion of his demesne called Ballyknock, which was then one of the most popular and best patronized gatherings in the province. All my friends induced me to enter her for the big race there, and I did so. When the day arrived, most of the people of the West went there to see what Maura could do, and to my horror as the time drew near for starting, my son, Joe Malley, who was to ride her, was blind drunk. I began scolding him, and a vast crowd gathered around us. A man forced his way through the crowd and said, 'Paddy, take it easy, I'll ride Maura-nee-Ortha for you.' Well, I looked at him then and I saw that he wore a caubeen with a green band around it. The colour and make of his clothes I couldn't tell, for he was enveloped in a dark green coat with a short back, but with skirts reaching the ground. Surely I was astonished at his cheek and was almost tempted to assault him, but yet I held my hand, for I well knew I had no other jockey, and the bell was clanging for the jockeys to be weighed.

" 'Very well,' I said, 'throw off your overcoat.' 'Not

I,' he said, 'these are my colours when I ride on the Curragh of Kildare.' The weighmaster ordered him to throw off his coat. 'Oh no,' he said, 'this is my livery, and you dare not object provided I am the proper weight,' said he, and he was the proper weight to the peel of an onion. Then he mounted Maura-nee-Ortha amidst the laughter of the crowd, and the next thing I heard was a shout, 'They're off!' There was a field of fourteen horses.

"When he had run about a furlong, my man pulled up Maura and galloped towards me and shouted, 'Get a jack-knife and cut off these skirts!' Many knives were pulled out by the crowd and the great skirts fell off in a jiffy and he flew off. He soon returned though, and then I knew I was ruined for life, for I had a good bit of money staked on the mare, as had hundreds from my parish. 'Here!' he shouted, 'sew on the skirts again. I'm no use without them.' How they were sewed on I don't know, for I was dazed, but they were sewed on; he flew off like the wind, followed by the laughter and execrations of the vast audience.

"There was an oblong hillock in the end of the field around which the course wound on the other side, and when the horses were just turning around the bend Maura-nee-Ortha rushed in among them. Then we lost sight of them for a minute or two, a time which seemed like an hour because of the silence and the tension, and then a horse came around the bend at the other end of the hillock and the hills reverberated with the shout that went up from the vast crowd as they shouted, 'Maura-nee-Ortha is first! She's coming with the speed of the wind!' Their wild huzzas rent the air, and sure enough it was she, and the people of the West who were there in hundreds shouted again and again, 'Hurrah! Hurrah for Maura-nee-Ortha, the glory and pride of the West!'

"On she came, her brave rider bending towards her ears, for there was a strong wind blowing against them and he knew well how not to retard her speed, and the tail of his great coat floated far behind him like the tail of a meteor rushing through space, and soon she rushed in past the winning post, and those who mocked them at the start were the most vociferous in their praise. There were two furlongs between her and the next horse, another bright bay mare, the property of Colonel Vandalure from the County of Clare. Then the man with the great coat dismounted and vanished, and from that day to this night I have never seen the man with the great coat who rode Maura-nee-Ortha that day to victory at Bally-knock."

"A CAKE" IN WEST MAYO

Down to the year of the great famine of 1846 a certain kind of social gathering in West Mayo was called "A Cake." Such events were of frequent occurrence throughout the various villages, and in a way they resembled patterns. They were something like the present-day raffles held to assist some worthy, struggling family, and were conducted with much decorum and politeness. Nor was there ever a row or a quarrel at such gatherings.

Supposing a poor family lost their only cow and had no earthly means of replacing her. The mother of the family went to some friendly publican and got from him on credit five or ten gallons of whiskey, some wine and cordials. She then went to a baker who baked her a great, ornamental cake about two or three stone in weight. Next she engaged the services of a musician; this was easily done, for the pipes in those days were as plentiful as blackberries in Autumn. The news was then spread abroad that "A Cake" would be held in a certain village on the next Sunday or holy day.

All the people of the surrounding villages would gather there in hundreds, decked out in their best holiday attire. All the marriageable peasant girls appeared in cashmere shawls and fine lace dress caps, garnished with nosegays and decorated with many ribbons of various shades and colours. There they would sit demurely and bashfully with the eyes of their ever-watchful mothers intent upon them. Vigilant as the mothers were, the bashful, blushing maidens sent many a wireless telegraphic message from their dark eyes to their favourite swains who sat in some distant corner.

The very last gathering of this kind was held in my native village on the Saint Patrick's day before the famine, and although I was then only about six years old, I have a clear and vivid recollection of it, for it was held quite near the cabin in which I was born. When I came on the scene all the people were gathered in a vast crowd, and the piper, a young man, sat on a chair in the open air playing "Haste to the Wedding." He was six feet four inches in height and admirably well-shaped, and was surely the most distinguished man I have ever seen, although he was blind.

This was Martin Moran, the son of a well-to-do farmer in the locality, considered to be the best player in Connacht in his day. It was a wonderful and glorious sight to

15

see him seated and playing, sometimes sweeping the keys of his pipes with great, long fingers. In after years when I had grown up, this masterful sweeping of his pipes filled my mind with visions of Carolan and the great and grand old harpers of ancient Erin. Martin became a great favourite of John McHale, the lion of Tuam, who presented him with a set of pipes which cost thirty-five pounds, and in presenting them the Archbishop christened Martin "the last of the Minstrels."

In front of the house there was a little sloping lawn in the centre of which stood a churndash, its handle driven firmly into the ground. On the upturned boss of the churndash was spread a white, home-made linen towel, on which was laid the great ornamental cake. The custom was that whoever carried in the cake should call for a round of drinks for the whole gathering. A young blacksmith of the town who was also a young man of property, one William Jordan, took in the cake and called for two gallons of punch, and wine and cordials for the ladies. Then the spree began in real earnest, and when it was over the woman was able to pay her creditors and to clear the price of a little cow as well, for cows were quite cheap in those days.

Among all the vast assembly at "the Cake" I noticed three old men who sat by themselves, and who in appearance and dress differed as much from those around them as the sun differs from the moon. These three noble-looking old men belonged to the eighteenth century and lived far into the nineteenth. They were the last of their generation I have seen, and their garb was of the best material that money could buy; in fact, it was the garb

16

of Henry Grattan, for the rich peasantry of their day affected the garb of the Upper Ten.

These three men were dressed alike; each of them held a fine top silk hat in his hand, and their hair which was cropped somewhat short grew luxuriantly on the crown of their heads, although I am sure they seldom combed it. Their high shirt-collars were of smooth home-made linen, and their cravats were black silk handkerchiefs brought twice around the neck and knotted carefully and neatly in front. Each wore a double-breasted, bottle-green broad-cloth coat and a double-breasted vest of the same material. They wore tight-fitting knee-breeches, and their legs were encased in brownish, olive-coloured box cloth, buttoned up to the knee leggings. Each of these clean-shaven men carried a polished, well-kept blackthorn stick with a gimlet hole near where they held it, through which was inserted a leather whang, both ends knotted together.

These three old men belonged to the faction-fighting days. When going into action they inserted the hand into the whang and pulled it up on the wrist. This was a wise precaution, for if they were struck on the hand by an antagonist, although they had to drop the stick, it still hung on the arm and they soon recovered it and returned to the fray. Some of the faction fighters went into battle armed with two sticks, one of which they used as a shield or buckler, while they assailed and struck with the other. They fought for glory, and sometimes for pleasure. They did not fight in order to kill; they did not use jack knives, stones or bars of iron like the other men of those times, for they were as honourable as Sarsfield, and as brave as Myles the Slasher.

One of these grand old men was a Mr. John David

Gibbons of Cloonlara, whose ancestors were the feudal kings of Glankeen. There he sat, stately even in his old age, with his distinctive, hereditary Roman nose, the hall-mark of the fine old clan to which he belonged. Next to him was a Mr. Walter James O'Malley of Furmoyle, who claimed to be descended not from Grainne, but from Doodarra O'Malley of the long ships, who lost his life while attempting to pillage the inhabitants of the dark blue Isles of Aran. The last man of this triumvirate was a Mr. O'Malley of Shraugh, who claimed to be descended from Mlaghlan fodda an rapier, that is, Malachie of the broad sword, who slew many of the Brownes of Westport who thought to seize his property. Spurred on by the desire for revenge, the first Lord Altamount offered his sister in marriage to any man who would fight and kill Mlaghlan in single combat. An English gentleman named Cox, who was considered the best swordsman in Europe, came over from London and challenged Mlaghlan. Tradition states that this Mr. Cox had a wooden leg.

On the day after his arrival, Cox drove out to Belclare with the Brownes, and on the road they met a man. "Who is that wonderful looking man whose hands reach below the knees and who carries his great sword in his left hand to keep it from clanging against the ground, and who is surely left-handed?" asked Cox. "That is the man you have challenged and will fight tomorrow," said Miss Browne, his prospective wife, and Cox seemed to tremble.

Next day they met in a historic field, the fatal field of Annagh where the pagan king of Killadangan and his worthless servant Thulera lie buried. With them sleep the twin sons of William O'Malley who fought here and ran each other through the body on account of a lady. On this day there was another grave to be filled on this field. Mlaghlan fodda an rapier and his clan were the first to arrive, and the Brownes, Cox and their plundering followers came soon after. The combatants threw off their upper garments and rolled up their shirt sleeves. There they stood beneath the shadow of Croagh Patrick, the Saxon and the Celt confronting each other. A clash of steel sounded in the terrible silence; then there came another clash of steel and yet another followed by a groan, for Mlaghlan had driven his terrible claymore to the hilt through the heart of the Saxon, and all was over. So Cox lies sleeping beside the Irish chieftains, wooden leg and all. Mlaghlan and his clan attacked the Brownes who fled the field, nor did they look behind them until they reached their stronghold which crowned the summit of Curranalurgan.

At "the Cake" there was present another man, a simpleton from birth, who always wore the cast-off clothes of a policeman. He belonged to the far West, but he made the town of Louisburgh his happy hunting ground. He was called Maurteen Omadaun, but he judged and settled a lawsuit which the County Court judge, the Judge of Assizes, and the parish priest had been unable to decide. This case was similar to the one in scripture, the one Solomon decided so wisely. The particulars are worth recording.

Until the famine time the small farmers along the sea coast sent their horses to summer grazing on the great hills which surround Doolough. These mountains are very precipitous, and on hot days the horses would stand on the brow of the cliff in order to inhale the cool breeze from the lake and to escape the stinging wasps. Then the eagles, with which these cliffs abounded, would swoop down upon them, dashing against their heads and striking the horses in the eyes with their strong pinions in order to make them restive and fall headlong to the dark glens below where the eagles could gorge themselves on their flesh.

In a certain village there were two men, each of whom had a mare with a filly foal at foot, and the two foals were alike in colour so that it was impossible to know one from the other. These two men sent the mares to graze on Mucelrea, the most precipitous of all the mountains. Like all the rest of the horses, the mares and their foals stood on the brow of a cliff and the eagles swooped down and drove one of the foals over the cliff to be dashed to pieces before it reached the bottom. Then the remaining foal began suckling both of the mares and continued to do so until the owners came for the horses; the question was to which mare did the foal belong, since she was suckling on both. There was much scolding and unpleasantness, and then the men went to law. When it reached the barrister at the Quarter Sessions, he could not decide the case. When it reached the Judge of Assizes, he was unable to decide, so he turned the matter over to the Parish Priest to arbitrate. His Reverence gave it mental thought and reflection, but he found that he was unable to solve the problem assigned to him and he was in a quandary, for he said that no man on earth could decide it.

One evening he was seated on a chair at the door of his neat, thatched cottage with a black velvet skullcap on his head, for he was aged and quite bald, when he saw Maurteen Omadaun go by. "Come here," he said, and the simpleton came to him. "Arra Martin avic," said the saintly old man, "did you hear that the case about the foal is left to my settlement?" "I did," said Martin. "Well then," said he, "it will fail me." "It is the simplest case on earth," replied the fool. "I would settle that case in five seconds." "Arra, Martin Grady, do you tell me so?" said the priest. "I do," said he. "Well then, Martin," said His Reverence, "I place the case in your hands." "Very well," answered the simpleton. "Send word to the men to take the mares and the foal into town tomorrow." "I will," said the priest.

The news spread that Maurteen was to arbitrate and deliver judgment the next morning on this peculiar, complicated case, so a great gathering took place of the townsmen and the people from the adjacent villages. In those days a great barrier or weir spanned the Louisburgh river some distance above the bridge; this weir backed up the stream and turned it into a large pond or reservoir whose northern shore was a level, sandy strand. This pool was called poolgorrive. "Take down the mares and the foal to the poolgorrive," ordered Maurteen. The people wondered at this command, but still they obeyed the mandate of the arbitrator and judge. "Now," said Maurteen, "place the mares on the strand with their heads to the water," and it was done. "Carry out the foal to the middle of the weir and cast him into the pond." Several men threw the foal into the pond.

When the foal came to the surface it began to neigh, and immediately one of the mares plunged into the water and swam towards the foal which she caught by the back of the neck and pulled ashore while the other mare took no interest in the proceedings. "The mare who saved the foal is its mother, for Nature has asserted itself," declared Maurteen, and the owners and all the people agreed with him, and they also asserted that Maurteen Omadaun had placed Solomon somewhat in the shade. Then they took him on their shoulders and carried him in triumph through the town.

This simple creature who proved to be so wise was supported all during his life by a wealthy matron of the town. Her husband owned a corn mill, and when the famine set in the mill was grinding corn day and night for the farmers who held their ground against the ravages of the blight. The farmers paid the owner in meal in lieu of cash. The stones or quarters of meal were turned to good account by the miller's grand old wife, for she got women to boil it into stirabout, and for three long and weary years she fed hundreds of starving people by day and night, and during all that time she saved many hundreds from death by hunger. May the shamrocks forever bloom and entwine above her grave, and the brightest sunbeams shine upon it. She often entertained Dives at her table, but she gloried in always having Lazarus as her honoured guest. Such was old Mrs. Paddy McGirr of blessed memory.

The three old men at "the Cake" seemed to take no interest whatever in the dancing and hilarity which surrounded them, for they were engrossed in a discussion of the old times. "Pat," said Walter O'Malley to the last of the packmen, "do you remember the Sunday we went to church, the Sunday the priest lent his flock to the parson in the year 1800?" "Indeed, I was one of them," said the packman. "I never heard about that," said Mr. Gibbons in great astonishment. "I will tell you all about it," said Pat.

"When the Protestant Church was built in Louisburgh, the first parson sent to occupy it was an Englishman named Vernon, a son of one of the oldest families in England, the Vernons of Hadden Hall. He fell in love with an actress and married her, so his friends disowned him and cast him off. When he arrived in Louisburgh, the Parish Priest, Father William Ward, became his inseparable friend, and each alternate day they dined with each other, and they took long walks, linked arm in arm. The poor young man, who once was senior wrangler in Cambridge University, had only three Protestants, one of whom was the sexton, in his congregation. Vernon wasn't long in town when the sexton, a married man, seduced the parson's wife and they decamped, leaving the parson covered by shame and humiliation. The priest pitied his forlorn condition.

"One day when returning from a long walk with the priest, the parson said, 'This is, I fear, our last walk, Father Ward.' 'Why?' asked the priest. 'Because my Bishop, that is Dr. Beresford, Bishop of Tuam, will be here on Sunday, and when he sees I have no flock he will close the church, and on next Monday I will be a homeless man and a wanderer.' 'Indeed you won't,' said the priest, 'for I won't have it.' 'How can you prevent it?' said the parson. 'Oh, quite easily,' replied Father Ward, 'for on next Sunday I will lend you my congregation. On that day when Mass is over I'll send my flock down to church to you, and believe me, old Beresford will be both charmed and astonished at beholding all your converts. Will that save you?' 'Oh, certainly it will,' said the parson.

"On Sunday when Mass was over, the priest took the congregation into his confidence and addressed them in their own simple manner of speaking, for there is no better way of arousing the sympathy of the Celt than to urge them to action in the dialect to which they are accustomed. 'Arra musha let ye all walk down to the crathereen and fill the church for him and sorra bit of harm it will ever do ye,' said His Reverence. 'The poor forlorn Kegriagh, let ye save him out of danger. It wasn't enough trouble for the deerough, his rip of a wife, to make off with old Hawkshaw, but now they will take the bit and sup out of the crathereen's mouth. Oh, wirra wirra go dea sho go dea schoch.' The whole congregation was moved to tears, and left the chapel and sailed down to the Protestant Church and filled it to capacity. The old bishop was charmed and declared they were the finest congregation he ever saw, and he dismissed them after giving his benediction. Ever afterwards the people prided themselves on the work of that Sunday, and they laughed and boasted at how they had fooled old Bishop Beresford, the Protestant Bishop of Tuam."

THE THREE DRUIDICAL SWORDS
OF CASEY

Midway between Old Head and the Killary, along the southern shore of Clew Bay, lies Lough Casey, convenient to the little village of Emlagh. It is an uninteresting sheet of water encompassed on all sides by monotonous scenery, but this insignificant lake has an interesting traditional history which is unique in the annals of Ireland. On the sandy shores of the lake there stood in a group firmly imbedded in the sand three tall lintels or flags about five feet high; these were called by the peasantry of the West the Clavie Choasagh, or the Swords of Casey. There they had stood since the days of the Firbolgs and the De Dananns, the menace and the terror of all the people who dwelt West of the Reek since the earliest ages and down almost to our day. There they stood, the Druidic Swords which since the days of the pagan ancestors slew some thousands of people; the terrific flags which immolated the powerful tyrants, the scandal-givers and the seducers. How on earth could these harmless looking flags slay or wound any man or woman? Here is how they did it, according to tradition.

Suppose a poor person was robbed and plundered by a tyrant, or suppose that an honest person was wrongfully accused of theft, or a virtuous female wrongfully accused of unchastity, there was no tribunal in the old or penal times to which they could appeal for justice and thereby vindicate their characters and reputations. Were they then to bear all this ignominy lying down, these peasants with their Celtic temperaments? Surely it would be hard to expect them to do this, and indeed they did not meekly submit to these injustices. As a last resort they appealed to the Swords of Casey, and, believe me, they got satisfaction, for the swords killed the tyrant or the traducer.

How was this done? First, the person who had been wronged fasted three days and nights and then went out to the swords and performed some kind of station around them, going the wrong way, and uttering some horrid incantation according to the liturgy of the Druids. Then this person knelt and upset the sand at the foot of the swords; immediately a tremendous cyclone swept the country, causing much damage to the peasantry, and at the same time the person who was responsible for the injustice of a diabolical accusation or deed against another fell dead, no matter where he or she chanced to be at the time.

About the year 1800 there lived in a certain village in the West a bailiff nicknamed the Plothy, and like all bailiffs we have ever seen, he was a heartless villain. In the same village with him there lived a young married couple just beginning the world, as they say, but it pleased God to call away the husband who died of a colic, leaving a widow and three children to weep. The bailiff swooped down and seized the dead man's little substance, leaving the young widow and her babes quite destitute, for he even took away their food. The woman became demented as she saw her children perishing of hunger, so she determined to appeal to the Swords of Casey. She fasted seventy-two hours and then she set out for the swords which were seven miles distant. She performed the curious station, concluding it by kneeling down and upsetting the sand. A cyclone swept through the country, and at that very moment the bailiff who was talking to a mason whom he had building a house, fell over on the scaffold. He began kicking and frothing as if in an epileptic seizure, and he expired shortly after being carried into his house.

This is the last case recorded in tradition, and it caused such a sensation that it reached the ears of the then Archbishop of Tuam, Dr. Skerrett, who determined to have a trial with the druidic swords. There was no Louisburgh in those days, for the ground on which it now stands was then all overgrown with white and black thorn and strewn with granite boulders. Since time immemorial it was in the Arcadian village of Aillemore that Confirmation was administered; consequently, there must have been some sort of a church there. In those days it must have been a very public place, although now it is one of the most unfrequented villages of the West.

When the summer winds began to blow, the Archbishop arrived in Aillemore. He hastened down to Lough Casey and assisted by his priests he dug up the swords. He then placed them in a boat and cast them into the middle of the lake, after which he returned in a jubilant mood to Aillemore. When he awoke the next morning, the first news he heard was that the Swords of Casey were standing firmly in their original position on the shore of the lake. The Archbishop put on his full pontificals, took his Crozier in his hand and marched down once more to Lough Casey. When he beheld the terrible pillar stones standing in the same spot he became enraged and ran towards them, smiting them with his Crozier until they fell. Then he took a sledge and smashed them into fragments, and taking the fragments into a boat, he rowed out to sea and cast them into the ocean where they sank beneath the dark waves and were never again seen on the shores of Lough Casey.

THE TRAGIC LOVE OF
JIMMY McDONOUGH

Should you chance to wander through Bunowen, a village on the southern shore of Clew Bay in West Mayo, the road which runs through it when it nears the sea branches off in two directions. One fork leads to the north and passes a neat, thatched cottage well sheltered by trees in which there lived some fifty years ago an amiable peasant named McEvilly. The other road runs towards the north-west by the door of a cottage surrounded by hawthorn trees, in which there lived a man named Berry, who was equally amiable. The reason why I have mentioned the names of men who now lie mouldering in their graves is in order to locate clearly where the hero of my story was born and raised.

Between these two roads, just where they branched off, a green, wedge-shaped little lawn sloped down to the crossroad, and on the little table-land at the head of this slope there stood for many generations a well-kept country house. It had an eastern aspect and commanded a fine view of Croagh Patrick and the great range of dark blue mountains which stretched away southwards to Killary Bay. In this house there lived in 1848 a family named McDonough consisting of nine children who were orphans, for both their parents died of famine fever in 1847, not through want or destitution, for they left a considerable sum of what the peasantry call dry money, and other means besides. There were six boys and three girls, almost all full-grown except two little chaps who were my juvenile comrades. They were all fair-haired, fair-skinned and freckled, and they were considered the best looking family in the half parish in which they lived. Their names were Jimmy, Owen, Pat, John, Affey, Martin, Ellen, Mary and Peggy.

Jimmy was a great favourite with the people and considered to be the finest young man West of the Reek. The colour of his hair was hard to define; it seemed to be either a light nut-brown or a delicate auburn shade, and it was short and curly to the top of his head. He had the sweetest and most sonorous voice of any mortal. I do believe he could read and write, and was great at figures. He was wonderfully well-shaped, as fleet as a wild deer, and he stood well over six feet. When he was called on to sing at the then frequent social gatherings, there would be a stampede towards the chamber where Jimmy was entertaining.

Just a mile from his home stood the little village of Toureen where there lived a poor peasant named Anthony Shiffell who had a full-grown family, one of them being a girl of twenty-two who was surely the most beautiful girl I have ever seen. Her father had no fortune to give her, but still she had great expectations, for it was well-known that certain relatives would give her a dowry of many thousands of pounds provided she got a rich man for a husband. Consequently, her parents and relations watched and guarded her every movement with the sleepless vigilance of Cerberus for fear she should choose her own partner for life. And yet somehow Maggie Shiffell fell desperately in love with Jimmy McDonough and he with her. It was the old, old story, and a silent war began to prevent a wedding.

The parents and relations who twigged it, as if by intuition, tried all sorts of stratagems to out-manoeuvre them, for although Maggie and Jimmy met once a week in the Shiffell home, Maggie was strictly guarded, and it took three long, weary years before the pair had the chance of meeting secretly. Of course, during these years the lovers did a fair share of telegraphy with the eyes and communicated their feelings in a hundreds and one little ways well-known to youths and maidens. Wise men inform us that those who wait patiently find what they wait for, and it came true in this instance.

On a certain Sunday in the glorious month of June, all the Shiffells went to a wedding, leaving Maggie to mind the house, moroya, but that was not their motive; they were afraid that she would elope with some boy who would be at the wedding. In the evening, Jimmy was on his way home from the house of a shoemaker who lived in the village of Moneen, and as he was passing Shiffell's door he heard Maggie calling him. "Conla of the golden locks, come in, I want you," she cried, and his heart gave a jump.

She was seated at the window holding a book in her hand with her index fingers between its leaves. He took it out of her hand and he saw that it was a great book she was reading, *The Imitation of Christ.* The peasant girls of those days never saw a magazine, a journal, a novel, or a penny novelette; consequently they became the best wives and mothers to be met on earth.

Maggie stood up to face him, and surely she was grand to look at. She was of medium height, and had nut-brown hair tinged with copper above the ears towards the temples from which the curls rose above her full and ample brow. Her eyes were dark blue, and her complexion was like a rose leaf. She wore a dark brown cashmere dress

30

with a tight-fitting bodice, and around her wonderfully white neck there stood a ruffle of white lace. This noble-minded girl was as wise as she was fair. "Now, Jimmy," she said, "we have got the chance we have long wished for; let us make good use of it, for it's our first and last chance. Let there be no frivolity between us. Let us understand each other now, once and for all, and proceed to arrange matters for the future. Believe me, we need to be quick, for the dark clouds are beginning to hover over me. Let us declare our feelings towards each other. Do you love me honestly and dearly?" "Oh, God knows that, and you ought to know it too," he answered fervently. "I do", she said, "but I wanted to hear it from your lips, and now listen to me. As great as your love is for me, my love for you is ten times greater. Be always ready, for if hard pressed I will fly to you, and then we will walk into the chapel and get married, and then we'll sail away to the land of the setting sun, and God will do the rest. And should we fail in a struggle for existence, and should I languish and pine away and die, my spirit will hover over you, and when you die I will meet you on the white strand of the world beyond. Then I will embrace and kiss you and we'll wander hand in hand together for evermore through the ever-green flowery meadows, the shady bowers, and the palm groves in the bright land of the blest."

She twined her hands around his neck, drew down his head and looked into his dark hazel eyes, and kissed him. "Now," she said, "our contract is sealed. That is the first kiss I have ever given to mortal man, and it shall be the last until you kiss me at the altar rail when I am your wedded bride." Then they parted, but they never saw each other again in this life.

Jimmy went home with his head in the air, the happiest man in Ireland. Some three weeks afterward the McDonough children were having tea in their well-kept little parlour when two of Jimmy's comrades came in and sat down. They were smiling and giggling. Jimmy was never afraid by night or day of either the living or the dead, but when he saw false friends smirking, a terrible fear caught hold of him. All his nerves became unstrung. "Any news, boys?" said Ellen McDonough to the pair of visitors. She was the oldest of the family and acted as mother to the orphaned children. "Did ye not hear it?" they asked. "No, what is it?" she replied. "That Maggie Shiffell got married this morning to some man from a distant parish," said one. "What is he like?" asked Ellen. "He is a large brute aged about fifty, and it's said he is pockmarked. They've gone off to his home," said the other.

Jimmy had the cup raised to his lips, and his hand began to shake as if he were stricken with palsy. His great fingers failed to hold the cup which fell on the saucer with a crash, shattering both pieces. This drew the attention of all the company towards him. There he sat, shaking violently from head to foot, and with his teeth chattering. "Oh, Jimmy dear, what ails you?" asked Ellen, but never a word did she get in reply. The false friends left hurriedly, for they saw they had almost killed him.

When night set in and the children were fast asleep in their beds, Jimmy arose and dressed himself in his Sunday clothes. He lit a rush lamp and placed it in the claw of the rude iron candlestick. Next he filled his powder flask and

32

filled his shotgun and placed it in position across his shoulders. On tiptoe he went to each bed and silently kissed his brothers and sisters. He opened the door and quickly latched it behind him, and he fled without a farthing in his pockets from all those he loved so dearly, his friends and relations, and the old ancestral home.

Next morning at dawn Ellen was awakened by hearing her two youngest brothers with whom Jimmy slept, calling out, "Where is Jimmy?" She sprang out of bed, but Jimmy of the golden curls and the wonderful voice was nowhere to be found, and the Celtic tale of the orphan children's wailing was wafted through the village. The villagers came running and gathered around them, but their sympathy availed little, for Jimmy, their glory and pride, had fled forever. The two old men whom I mentioned at the beginning of this story, McEvilly and Berry, saddled their horses and went in search of him, for what Mat Donovan was to the people of Knocknagow, Jimmy McDonough was to the people of Bunowen. Alas, they never found him, although they inquired all along the road to Castlebar where they went thinking that he might have gone there and enlisted. Some time afterwards a man wrote from England stating that he saw Jimmy in a Dragoon regiment, but this tale turned out to be untrue. Another neighbour named Devany wrote home saying that he saw him in Philadelphia, and this aroused the McDonough children who determined to emigrate.

Ellen and Mary began baking much oatmeal bread and laying up a stock of butter for the voyage, for the company who owned the "coffin ships" did not give the emigrants one-fifth of the food supply needed for the voyage. When all was ready, the children cast open the doors of their ancestral home and left it derelict. They abandoned the farm they had made productive and fertile by the sweat of their brows, and others of the village did the same so that the landscape was disfigured with the derelict, ruined homes of the peasantry, and their deserted farms lay fallow. Nor had the peasantry who remained the courage to occupy them, for as a result of all they had seen and gone through during the time of the famine, they thought the end of the world was at hand.

The McDonough children and many more of the peasantry of the West went on board a brig named the "William Barrington" in Inishlyre and sailed down Clew Bay. The peasantry gathered in hundreds to bid a last farewell to the relations and friends they would never again see on earth. They mounted the hill of Old Head, some of them carrying huge bundles of straw which they would light on the cliffs as the brig bore down on the wild headland. When the ship drew near, they lit some of the straw and began shouting. Some of the females shrieked and gesticulated wildly, and as the brig was passing they ran along the tremendous cliffs to light more straw on the brow of the cliff of Derrylahan. Then they rushed westward and set more straw blazing on the summit of Fairy Hill. Next they crossed the Bunowen river, ran along the strand and climbed the hill of Carramore. As the brig passed quite near this hill they began shouting, calling their relatives by name, and setting ablaze the last bundles of straw. Wailing and weeping, they threw themselves on the ground and watched the brig until she disappeared below the western horizon; then many of the females swooned and had to be carried home.

I was just eight years old at the time, and took part in

the demonstration of grief on Fairy Hill as the McDonough children sailed away. A giant nicknamed Tommy
Paddagh swung me on his back and ran madly into the
crowd, crossed the river and along the strand of Carramore, and then climbed the steep hill and placed me on
its summit. I shall forever remember that terrible scene.
Ah, it's many and many a steep hill and high mountain
I have climbed since then, but the memory of that night
of grief and mourning on the hill of Carramore is deeply
embedded in my heart.

Later we learned the details of the voyage of the brig
"William Barrington" to America. When the coffin-ship
reached mid-ocean the emigrants began to die, for the
hold in which they were confined had no ventilation and
became as hot as an oven, turning it into a death hold.
The youngest of the McDonough orphans, Affey and
Martin, were among the first to die and be buried at sea;
this slaughter of the innocents continued until they almost
reached the land. After a journey of nineteen long and
weary weeks, the brig reached America where she vom-
ited out from the hold the emaciated, half-starved white
slaves, or all that remained of them, into the city of
Philadelphia. From that day until the last of the family
died, the McDonough children never again saw their
darling Jimmy of the golden hair.

And what was Jimmy's beloved Maggie doing all during this time? When the giant took her to his enchanted
castle, she was morbid. She sat down in her room, her
hands in her lap, and there she sat staring at nothing, ap-
parently. She was looking inward at her lost love with
the eyes of her mind, however, and for eleven months she
continued in that position, for she had lost all interest in

life. At the end of that period the pangs of child labour set in, but she had no strength to bring forth the baby, nor did she realize her condition. She never called for help, so she died where she knelt beside her bed, and the great marriage match that had been made for her ended in dust and ashes. How this phenomenal marriage was brought about, no person could or did find out; surely some supernatural power had been at work to overthrow her love and destroy her life. Those who were the human agents who caused her death and turned the McDonough orphans into exiles and sent two of them to the bottom of the wild Atlantic, will surely have a bad half hour when they stand before the judgment seat of God.

JIMMY McDONOUGH'S FLIGHT TO CONNEMARA

When Jimmy McDonough fled from his home and kindred, he determined to reach some country where he could hide himself and never be traced, and he knew where that country lay. Just beside the house in which he was born and near the cabin in which I first saw the light of day, there dwelt an old peasant with thin, aquiline features, a man who was blind in one eye and who had a great blue scar on his high, full, narrow brow, for he was an old rebel who fought at the battle of Castlebar and received these two wounds at the battle of Ballinamuck. When I used to look at him and whenever memory brings him before my mental vision, I used to then and ever since think of Hannibal.

The old man's name was Jimmy Malley, but he was

always called by the nickname "Go-go" which he won in his escape from Ballinamuck. He remained in Southern Connemara, which was then the wildest portion of Ireland, for twenty-five years, supporting himself as a quack doctor, for in those days the medicine man was in high repute among the wild, simple natives. When he was quite an aged man, he returned to his native village of Bunowen and was astonished to find his wife still living and his family, consisting of three daughters and a son, fully grown and in comparative comfort. They received the old, veteran patriot with open arms, nor was he in his old age ever afterwards heeded by the Government.

This old man's house after his return from exile, when I was a child, was during the winter nights the favourite rendezvous of all the youths and maidens of the village, as well as of the wee chaps, for Jimmy was forever recounting his adventures and dangers both in field and flood, and we small chaps used to pray fervently that he would never cease these tales. He was forever describing the wild land of his exile, its almost interminable moors and swamps, the thousands of lakes, sluggish mountain streams and roaring torrents of a land without roads, paths or trails, a rough granite-strewn region which abounded in caves, a land where the king's writ never ran, and where never a word of English was uttered. When the refugee reached this region he was received with open arms by the primitive natives who were as true as steel, and he was as safe as if he had taken refuge in the moon.

The natives were as primitive in their manners and customs as our ancestors were a thousand years ago. They had many faults, but most of their faults and failings leaned to virtue's side. The males from earliest boyhood, like our pagan ancestors, delighted in athletic sports, especially hurling and wrestling, which their descendants still continue to engage in every Sunday of the year on the sandy beaches along the seashore. When these lads become full-grown they excel as wrestlers. About eight years ago, a young man named Pat Connolly from the vicinity of Carna in Connemara, went off to Scotland, carrying with him his fame as a wrestler. When he reached Glasgow he was picked up by a Sporting Club which took him on a tour through the principal cities of the British Isles, and no man he met ever threw him on the mat. For the past two years he has journeyed through the United States and Canada, and he has never met there a man fit to throw him, so he now claims to be the world's champion wrestler. He is a splendid young man, a native of Connemara, and surely a credit to his land.

When Jimmy McDonough closed the door of his ancestral home behind him and fled from Bunowen, he determined to reach Southern Connemara, the region where old Malley had found refuge, and hide there forever. He placed his gun on his arm and set his face to the South, nor did he ever look around him until he reached Doolough. He sat down in a little glen beside that terrible spot in the goat track which overhangs the dark lake called the Stroppabue. The little glen slanted down to the cliff, and was thickly overgrown with tall, wide-leaved, wild fern which grew luxuriantly above the graves of his much-wronged, famished countrymen who had perished in this desolate pass some three years before, a dreadful tragedy which might well be called the slaughter of the innocents.

DEATH AT DOO LOUGH

In the spring of 1847, some six hundred of the starving peasantry of the West thronged into the town of Louisburgh, seeking food or a ticket for admission to the workhouse from the Relieving Officer. He informed them that he had no power to give them food or a ticket, and that they should apply personally to the two paid guardians, a Colonel Hograve and a Mr. Lecky, who would hold a board meeting the next day in Delphi Lodge, Bundorragha. The Lodge was situated in the wildest, uninhabited region in Ireland, eighteen miles distant from the proper boardroom at Westport, and ten miles distant from Louisburgh. This was a deliberate trap set up by the Government of that day in order to decoy the starving Celts out to this wild region in order to slaughter them.

These six hundred people had no homes to return to; they were in rags, almost naked, and they had not tasted any kind of food for days, so severe was the famine. They sat down in front of the houses in Louisburgh during that night, and many of them were found stark dead where they lay next morning. On that day some four hundred of them arose shivering in their rags, all barefooted and still without food; they sighed and looked up to heaven before setting out on a journey from which none of them was to return.

When they reached Glankeen, they had to wade through the river which was swollen by recent rains. Their rags from the hips downward were saturated with water on that cold, damp day. When they reached the southern bank of this rapid mountain torrent, there was nothing even resembling a road between that spot and

39

Doolough, so that they had to negotiate the dreadful goat track along the brow of the precipice which overhangs the house of the late Captain Houstan. They encountered another river far deeper than that of Glankeen, and since there were no bridges in those days they had to battle their way through the stream, with the result that they were wet to the waist.

When the wet and suffering peasantry reached Delphi Lodge, the vice-guardians were at lunch and could not be disturbed, so the people sat down in their damp, miserable rags among the pine trees, and there many of them expired. When the two gentlemen condescended to see the peasantry, they refused to grant them relief or tickets to the workhouse, so the fearful journey had been all in vain.

Night was now approaching and ten long, weary miles of a wild, uninhabited region lay between them and that land where once had stood their happy homes. Now they were homeless, and with despair in their hearts they set out once more for the place of their birth. When they reached the river where Houstan's house now stands, they once more had to wade through it, saturating their rags anew. The wind veered around to the north-west bringing a storm with showers of piercing hailstones. Their wet rags began to stiffen like cold sheet iron around their emaciated limbs, and soon they began to fall and die along the rough path, or to fall in their weakness into the lake below.

When they reached that terrible spot called the Stroppa-bue, on the very brow of the cliff, the tremendous squalls swept them by the score into the lake, and those who were trying to climb the steep-slanting pass or stroppa, lost their hold and fell as they climbed. The corpses which fell into the lake were never recovered. The few who survived the struggle through the Stroppa-bue continued to fall and die until the last of them perished on the southern bank of the Glankeen river. On the next morning the trail from Glankeen to Houstan's house was covered with corpses as numerous as the sheaves of corn in an autumn field. There is nothing in Irish history to equal this horrible butchery, nor is there anything in the history of Europe to equal it in horror, save the tragic retreat of Napoleon's army from Moscow.

On the following day, the Relieving Officer took gangs of starving men with him from Louisburgh along the corpse-strewn trail, and they buried the slaughtered peasants without coffins just where they fell. When they reached Doolough there was no earth along the goat track deep enough for graves save in the little glen or ravine which ran down to the brow of the cliff, and which frowns above the dark lough just beside the terrible Stroppa-bue. So they had to gather all the corpses and carry them to the little glen where they buried them in pits just as on a battlefield, and there they lie sleeping where the sighing of the winds through the tall, wild ferns which wave above their nameless graves forever sings their requiem.

It was in this lonely glen in which so many of his former neighbours lay buried that Jimmy McDonough of the golden hair and the wonderful voice sat down to rest at midnight, unconscious of the savage, lonely scenery which surrounded him. His thoughts were turned to Connemara, that unknown region to the south, towards

41

which he fled to escape the memories of his home and his shattered love.

THE ROLLING STONE OF LETHER BRICKAWN

As Jimmy McDonough sat at midnight in the lonely glen at Doolough where many of his former neighbours were buried, wondering what awaited him in his journey to Connemara, he was suddenly aroused from his lethargy by the shrill cry of a woman wafting its frightening way through the ravines of the ominous mountains. A cold thrill ran down his spine as he sprang up and fled along the rocky goat track, nor did he look behind him until he reached Bundorragha. The inhabitants of the well-sheltered, ancient hamlet were fast asleep as he went out on the quay and unmoored a boat. He took an oar in each hand and pulled vigorously across beautiful Killary Bay. When he reached the Galway side of the bay he securely moored the boat, fore and aft. He sprang out and climbed the rugged hill of Derry-na-Clough, and turning his face to the South, he sat down on a rock at the summit.

For the first time in his life he beheld the Irish Alps, the far-famed Banabola mountains, stretching away as straight as an arrow from the banks of the Corrib in the East to the shore of the wild western Atlantic, dividing the vast mountainous barony of Ballinahincha into two evenly divided halves. There they stood in their glory, all radiant and gorgeously decked out in their many-coloured summer holiday attire of purple-green and yellow, their white peaks shining with a silvery sheen as the early sun-rays glistened upon them. How to pass through or over these peaks was the problem which confronted Jimmy. But he was a resolute, lithe, vigorous young man who never was daunted by anything, so he determined to climb them, hoping that he would die in the effort, though not by his own hand, for he grieved deeply for his lost love.

Jimmy stood up and descended the southern slope of the rugged hill to traverse the green vale of Glencroff through whose centre there flows a charming river with low, verdant banks. As he crossed over this river he thought of Homer and the Scamander. When he finally emerged from the valley, some five miles of heath-covered moors lay between him and the Banabolas. As he advanced, he roused a covey of grouse and shot two of them which he took with him. He soon reached a deserted village called Letter-shan-balla which stood on the western slope of a heather-clad hill, a village whose inhabitants all perished of hunger some three years before.

When he reached the great monarch of the eastern range of the Banabolas, the stupendous Maamturk mountain which stands on the eastern shore of beautiful Loch Inagh, he met another deserted village nestling in a crevice beneath the northern base of the mountain; this place was called Lether Brickawn, and it was now abandoned, for all of its inhabitants had died of hunger. Here Jimmy lingered, for this ruined little hamlet had a history. When inhabited, it belonged to the parish of Ballinakill about the year 1825 or 1830.

The parish priest of Ballinakill and his two curates used to hold a confession station in the now deserted village.

43

One of the curates was a young man of great strength and stature who was reputed to be the cleverest young priest in the Archdiocese of Tuam for, through his mother he inherited natural talent, eloquence and fluency both in Irish and English, for she belonged to the O'Malleys of Curragaun, a village near the mouth of the Killary. The O'Malleys were the wealthiest and most eloquent stock who ever figured West of the Reek.

The young curate was Father James O'Malley of Cahir, a village just beside the little town of Louisburgh. When Archbishop McHale was translating Homer and Moore, one of the priests anonymously attacked him in the newspapers of that day, and the letters were as galling to the Archbishop as the letters of Junius were to those they were aimed at, but the Archbishop could not learn the identify of his attacker. He called together all the priests of the Archdiocese of Tuam, but again he failed to find the identify of the culprit.

"Well, now," said His Grace, "the enquiry is over and there are only two men among you fit to write such able letters. No man ever wrote those letters but you, James O'Malley, or you, Joe Burke." Father Joe Burke was then a young curate in Louisburgh. "Well, Your Grace," said Father Joe, "it is I who wrote the letters; give me my exeat and I will leave your diocese." So he received it and went off to America. I have given this anecdote in order to show how clever Father O'Malley was and the opinion His Grace had of him. Big Father James O'Malley of Cahir is, I daresay, quite forgotten in his native parish, but not by me. He lies buried on the bright, sunny slope above the holy well of Kilgeever, with a Celtic Cross above him guarding the handful of brown clay which

44

was once a very distinguished, intellectual priest.

When the confession station was ended in the little village of Lether Brickawn on that day years ago, the priests, as was usual in those days, remained for dinner. Father James O'Malley determined to climb the tremendous Maamturk mountain which overhung the little hamlet. Yet, it is easier to climb than Croagh Patrick, although it is far steeper. This mountain was covered with heath and wild mountain grass, and it was generally cloud-capped. When Father James reached the summit, he saw an enormous granite rock on the very brow of the mountain. At the least this rock was two or three hundred tons weight, and it rested on a bank of red clay. Since the earliest ages the sheep, goats and other animals used to shelter beside it in winter time, and in summer they used to seek its shade. They were forever scraping and scratching themselves against the bank on which the rock rested, so that as time went by they wore away the clay, undermining two-thirds of the base.

Father James saw that the rock was sure to fall with the first rain or frost of the winter, and without a thought of the little village which lay below the hill, he determined to dislodge the stone for fun's sake. He lay on his back, placed his feet against the rock, and with might and main he gave a shove. Like some pre-historic, monstrous animal aroused from its lair, the dreadful rock sprang into life, and bounded down the side of the mountain, driving a torrent of stones and pebbles before it. As it sprang and collided against other rocks, the echoes rang out with the shock of the impact.

The priest had forgotten the village, and as he searched the spot on which the rock had stood, he saw a bull's horn embedded in the clay. It occurred to him that in olden times the horn must have been shoved in through a rat or weasel hole. When he picked up the horn to examine it, he found within it twenty-five gold guineas.

Meanwhile, the villagers had been sitting below on a hillock inhaling the sweet perfume which was wafted towards them from the station house by the mild zephyrs, for the air was redolent with the aroma of roasting and boiling. All too soon they were aroused from their pleasant occupation by the sound of a dreadful crash high above them. Startled, they looked up and saw death rushing down towards them. With might and main they ran for dear life towards a foothill. On came the rock, springing and bounding, gaining impetus as it descended and soon, as if in a fury, it sprang into the doomed little village of rude stone cabins, and it took three of the houses with it into the deep, swampy glen at the foot of the mountain.

When Father James descended the hill, singing one of the old tunes, he found the village in ruins and the natives lamenting. The wild, sad Irish wail of the homeless matrons rent the air, but the priest was not astonished at the ruin he had caused, for he sprang from a race that never wondered at anything. He raised his hands and bade the people to be silent. "Ah, my friends," he said, "be of good cheer. It was God who put it in my mind to cast down the stone, for it was sure to fall next winter, perhaps when ye would be gathered at breakfast or dinner, or when sleeping at night in your beds, when ye would be sure to be killed. See what I found under the rock," and he showed them the horn and the gold. "This will build new homes for you, far better than the ones you have lost."

46

So he divided the contents of the horn among them, and went off to dinner.

Then the villagers went to work with a will and soon three new homes arose like phoenixes out of the ruins. They were the envy of the other villagers, for such, alas! is human nature; some of the inhabitants prayed fervently that Father James on his next visit would roll down another rock and find another bull's horn full of gold in order that they, too, might build more up-to-date mansions.

THE BAILIFF AND THE BLACKSMITH

In the winter of the year 1825 all the peasantry who dwelt along that portion of the southern shore of Clew Bay which stretched westward from Old Head to Emlagh, were gathering seaweed in a full storm which was blowing from the northwest, accompanied by terrible showers of hailstones. The sea was in a fury as it lashed against the headlands, and the clouds seemed to be surcharged with electricity as the heavens were illumined by great flashes of lightning. The thunder crashed and shook the universe, rolling and rumbling as it died away in the distance.

About noonday as the toiling workers looked in the distance across the angry ocean they beheld a great ship coming in the sound which separates Clare Island from Achill, and they plainly saw that she was in distress. When she weathered the northern point of Clare Island at Carramore, the wind veered around some points towards the north, with the result that the ship was driven towards the west. It became evident to the watchers that she was heading for Polgloss, a little village which lies nestling at the foot of the western slope of the hill of Carramore.

All those who were working along the shore ran towards the little village. On she came, the noble ship, her white sails torn and streaming in the storm as she ran before the wind. Sometimes the watchers would lose sight of her as she sank buried in the trough of the sea between the breakers, but then she would appear once more, raised high on the white crest of a great roller, only to fall headlong with a crash almost on her beam ends, once more lost to view. On came the gallant ship, fighting and battling through the raging ocean towards the shore.

There were wild hurrahs from the crowd on land as the ship drew nearer and nearer. Suddenly, a strange thing happened, for the crew who were gathered in the bows of the vessel threw a cabin boy overboard into the raging breakers. Some brave men in the crowd of watchers caught each other's hands and waded out towards the little lad who was swimming weakly towards them, and they carried him safely to land. The great ship was lifted on high by the ground swell and driven headlong into the shingly beach or dourlin. The sailors were exhausted, but when they recovered they told their sad story.

Some two months before, while they were at sea, the captain lost his bearings and the ship had been wandering ever since. During those dreadful days they had not once glimpsed the sun or the stars. When windward of the Bills a wave struck the vessel and carried away the wheel-house together with the captain who was steering the ship. When asked why they cast the cabin boy overboard, they said they thought they were approaching some part of the coast of Africa, and they feared the crowd on shore might be savages who would murder them. In order to test the crowd they threw the boy overboard, for if the people tried to save him they were sure to be Christians, but if they didn't try to save him they were sure to be savages. As the crew told their story the tide was receding, and in a short space of time the ship stood high and dry, nor was she much injured. She was laden with oranges packed in boxes. In the evening, each man of the crowd took home with him a box of oranges.

At that time the Brownes of Westport had a bailiff in Louisburgh, an Orangeman from the North who hated the Catholic peasantry and did them much harm, but he detested above all of them four men, one of whom was a blacksmith. The bailiff took charge of the ship until the arrival of the Coastguard, at which time he took some of the Coastguard with him to search for the boxes which the peasantry had taken away. This was a pretext to ruin his four enemies, for he began with them first of all. He tore down their gerlings of potatoes in their barns and let them loose over the threshed oats; he tore down their turf-stacks and their ricks of hay as well as all the stacks of corn and cocks of straw. In fact, he almost put them out of house and home, but then like a fool he attacked the blacksmith's property, and he even smashed his furniture.

The blacksmith when roused to fury was relentless and unforgiving, and he swore a terrible oath that he would see this business through to the bitter end. Everyone who knew the smith realized that it would be a fight to the finish. The smith fasted three days and three nights before he went out to his forge and took hold of his hereditary sledge, for he was a hereditary smith. He began to smith

49

the cold, naked anvil, and the anvil began to roar until it rang out through the little town and the sound was heard in the adjacent villages. The peasantry knew from traditional instinct what was on, and the roar of the anvil as he smote it had something human in it, for it was like the roar of some gigantic mortal in the death agony. This diabolical thing was much dreaded by the Irish peasantry. From the earliest times they called it gratha, an inune, that is, the thrashing of the anvil.

The people who heard the anvil roaring were much perturbed and retired early to bed that night. Next morning when they arose the news spread like luska sleiva that Jimmy Blain, the terrible bailiff, was a corpse. He was found sitting up in bed, his eyes wide open as if glaring at some fearful object, his teeth set rigidly, and his two hands grasping the bedclothes as if trying to strangle some demon. The news soon reached the three countrymen whose homes he had ruined. "No," said one of them, "I will never believe it until I see the house fly walking on his dead face and going into his nostrils." So they went to the wake where they saw the house flies on his face, and the incredulous one went home satisfied. I knew the smith, who died of a colic in 1848, but the other three men whom the bailiff ruined lived on until I was a young man, and I have heard them telling this story a hundred times. I never heard them describe the roaring of the anvil but I thought of Lia Fail or Stone of Destiny which roared beneath the monarchs of ancient Erin at their Coronation.

HUGH GORDON,
THE "JUMPER" OF FEENONE

Beneath the north-eastern slope of Mweelrea, a wild mountain in West Mayo, lies the sequestered village of Feenone which is far-famed for the fertility of its soil and the industry of its inhabitants who seemed to resemble the two races of mankind whom Gulliver met in his travels. But if they differed in physique they excelled as husbandmen, having at all times and seasons an abundance of the necessities of life. At eventide in summer when the village maidens sat milking their cows on the slope of the great hill which overhung the hamlet, or along the verdant banks of the river which placidly glides through it, their jocund songs filled the vale with melody which denoted to the passing stranger that they were a happy and contented peasantry. The feathered songsters seemed to vie with the milkmaids, for the melodious voice of the cuckoo resounded amid the cliffs and ravines of the mountains; the thrushes gushed forth their joyous songs in dark hazel bowers; blackbirds were whistling in the evergreen holly; the corncrakes were calling in the meadows and cornfields which sloped down to the limpid stream, and the linnets and other little warblers were twittering on the brambles. Such was the village of Feenone in the old times, but alas, I fear the hand of time has now despoiled and denuded it of much of its former embellishment, its charming sylvan scenery.

The townland was laid out in rundale, a system which is much criticized and condemned by modern writers who pose as experts, and who would have the people believe that it arose from or as a result of the ignorance of our ancestors, but if we inquire into the system we find that the opposite is the fact. Let us suppose that twelve men rented a vacant townland in order to build a village in which to live; we, of the present day, might think they should divide the land into twelve strips and then cast lots for them. But then perhaps six of the men might have very good strips, while the others might have very bad ones. Since this would be against the rules of fair play, how did they divide the townland? They divided it according to the Brehon Laws laid down by Cormac McArt, making three parts of the townland, that is, the very best land, the middling land, and the worst land. Then they made twelve parts of the best land and cast lots in order that each would have a portion of the good land, and they followed the same procedure for the middling land and the poor land. The reader can see how fair, honest and unselfish our ancestors were in dealing with each other. Nor does this denote ignorance. There were no fences except upright stones here and there to mark the mearings, and when the peasants harvested the last of their crops in November, the townland was common to all of the inhabitants until the following April.

The great hills which overhung the village and the vast moors which surround it were rent free and common to all the people the whole year round. This was the rundale system which came down to us from our pagan ancestors, and it exists on some estates where I now dwell down to this day. Strange to say, there was scarcely ever a dispute among the people over this system, but, of course, there is seldom a rule without an exception. I have gone into detail about this system in order that the reader may understand my story which, if rudely put together, is surely a sad one, a story which arose from a trivial cause and caused the ruin of a happy family, a story which need never have been told if the chief actor in it had obtained fair play and justice. Nor would I record this story now if any of the relatives of the leading character were now alive, but they are not, for the sept to which he belonged has been extinct in the male line for over half a century.

In that Arcadian village of Feenone there lived about the year 1830 a very respectable man named Hugh Gordon, a small farmer and a blacksmith. Since time immemorial, all his ancestors who dwelt in Carramore were hereditary smiths, and they were considered to be one of the most ancient tribes West of the Reek. The males of every generation seem to have been few in number, but the females became the ancestresses of one-third of the peasantry West of Old Head. Hugh Gordon was tall of stature, wonderfully broad-shouldered, and hideously pock-marked. Unfortunately for himself, he was a good scholar, considering the age in which he lived; in fact, he was a far better-informed man than any man of his class and status of the present age, but he lacked what he most needed in life, namely, patience and fortitude in bearing up against a wrong and an injustice.

About the year 1830, a dispute arose between Hugh and a neighbour as to the ownership of one of the little patches of ground. I dare say that since there were no fences the boundary marks may have become obliterated. Of course, there was much scolding and unpleasantness, and the two contestants went to law, but when the county chairman failed to settle the case, he sent it back to the Parish Priest to arbitrate it. The P.P., a Father Gibbons, was quite an old man, almost in his second childhood, who thought very little of a small bit of land in far-away Feenone, so without a thorough investigation he decided against Gordon, although it is quite certain that the land belonged in fact to Gordon. Twenty years afterwards, when Gordon's name was on every tongue, I heard all the old men of the region declare that the land belonged to Gordon.

Hugh Gordon came of a race who never forgot or forgave, a silent race. When Sunday came around, he dressed himself in his best clothes and walked to Louisburgh where so many of his relations then lived. When he reached the square, he turned to the left and walked down to the Protestant Church and became "a jumper" in order to spite the priest, moryagh, and so his doom was sealed. He had committed a crime and a sin against nature, for he had done a thing which was unheard of in that western region since the time when Saint Patrick prayed and fasted on the summit of the blessed Reek; all during that long period of fourteen hundred years a western peasant was never known to desert the faith of his fathers. For wasn't it the peasantry, the class to which he belonged, who kept the Catholic faith alive in Ireland from the days of Elizabeth down to the days of O'Connell, and who supplied most of the priests who guided the people on towards heaven? The grand, heroic priests of penal times were sons of the same peasants who were smuggled off to Spain to be educated and ordained and then returned to Ireland, determined to lay down their lives for the faith of their fathers. May it be always remembered that if the keeping of the faith lay with the Irish aristocracy and gentry, the Catholic faith would have long since vanished, for the gentry of Irish descent gave up the faith much sooner than those of English descent, in order to retain their estates, or in order to grab those of their neighbours. For instance, the O'Malleys of Belclare and of Murrisk "jumped" and became Protestants sixty-two years before the Brownes of Westport became Protestants. The last of the packmen of the West often told me that his uncle, Owen O'Malley of old Cahir-na-Mart, who reared him, frequently told him that he attended Mass in a large, barn-like structure which stood on the top of the hill of Carra-lurgan, and that it was one of the Brownes of Westport who used to serve Mass there, a young gentleman named Peter Browne Kelly, so we can see that the apostasy of the Brownes is of recent date.

When Hugh Gordon left the Protestant Church that Sunday morning, he found to his cost that he had severed all connection with his nearest and dearest friends and relations, as well as with the peasantry of the West. He had dug a chasm, a gulf, that could not be bridged over. He had done an unnatural deed, and now the people feared him as if he had suddenly become possessed by a devil; in fact, they suddenly became afraid of their lives of him as if he were some terrible man who had risen from the grave. As he walked down Bridge Street, Louis-burgh, he saw all the doors closed against him; when he crossed the bridge and began to wend his way home-wards, all those he overtook crossed themselves and fled through the fields or bogs, and those who were coming towards him did the same, for they were afraid of his pock-marked face.

When he reached his home in Feenone, he saw all the villagers blessing themselves and rushing towards their houses, and now he realized that he was a ruined man.

Never, oh never, was he to hear their friendly voices welcoming him to their bright firesides. Never, oh never again would he feel the pressure of their friendly hands, for he had done a deed on that day which was unheard of in that region, and they were determined never more to associate with him. For a month he remained at Feenone as if in prison, and the loud, familiar clang of his anvil was hushed and stilled. Then he cast the doors of his once happy home open to the winds and fled to England. The outraged peasantry heaved a sigh of relief, for they imagined that they were rid of him for ever.

For twenty years Gordon remained in England until he was quite forgotten in his native parish. Then the great famine began. At that time there were fifteen hundred families in the Parish of Louisburgh, Kilgeever Parish, which was then thickly populated. It had a coastline which extended from Kilsallagh to the Killary, and from its mouth to Aasleagh at the head of the beautiful little bay, and every valley, glen and dell of that vast, mountainous region was thickly populated. One-third at least of the inhabitants were squatters, conacre men, who had no land or means whatever. When the potato, their staple food, failed, their doom was sealed. The first year of the famine they perished with hunger at the rate of at least two hundred persons each week. Then the mild, amiable parish priest lost heart, or at least his courage, for I dare say he thought the end of the world was at hand, so he asked for his exeat and fled away to far-off Buenos Aires in South America, leaving his perishing flock and poor old weeping Erin far behind him. When the famine cloud had rolled away, carrying with it two or three millions of the Irish peasantry, the old priest caught his courage with both hands and returned to the now denuded Isle of Destiny whose once emerald surface was now disfigured by the skeletons of ruined houses, and the nameless graves of his famished countrymen. It was assumed that he would never get a living from the great John McHale of Tuam, but it turned out otherwise, for shortly after his return he was quietly installed as P.P. of Clifden. When the old priest fled at the end of the first year of the famine, he was replaced by the much admired and respected Father Tom McCaffrey, a Westport man, who unfortunately was a chronic invalid suffering from consumption. Soon after his appointment, he lay down on his bed in Tooreen, never to leave it again until he was carried to his grave in the old chapel of Louisburgh.

This critical time was the golden opportunity for the Irish Church Mission, the Protestant organization. They grasped their opportunity, and after a twenty years' absence they let loose Hugh Gordon among the starving peasantry of his native parish. He was accompanied by a strange parson and a large staff of scripture readers and ranting preachers, who came to preach the Word, as they called it. They looked around in order to choose a site on which to build the new Jerusalem, and they chose the village of Bunlehinch which lay along the northern margin of the charming vale of Cloonlara in the centre of the parish. The village was inhabited, but the then Marquis of Sligo was accommodating. To his eternal shame, he evicted the villagers and handed over Bunlehinch to the Irish Church Mission whose members began to build the colony, or new Jerusalem, at a great rate, and phoenix-like it soon rose out of the ashes of the ruined village.

A neat cottage was built for the manager, Gordon, the

new Mahomed of the West, and soon there appeared a church with a schoolhouse, and a long street of cottages for the " 'verts". The cottages were soon filled, for hunger is a great leveller. When hunger comes in by the door, pride and shame fly out through the window. But even if some of the starving peasantry lost their pride and shame, they didn't lose the faith of their fathers. Gordon was cock of the walk, tricked out in the garb of a minister of the Gospel, and the air was filled with the ringing of bells and the singing of vespers.

Still, Gordon's lust for converts was unsatisfied. He determined to start an auxiliary colony, and of all the places in the parish he chose Bunowen, not that he expected converts there, but in order to annoy the parish priest who then lived in Bunowen. When Father McCaffrey died, he was succeeded by the venerable, saintly Father Myles Sheridan, another Westport man, who took up his abode in Bunowen. About the time when Father Sheridan was appointed, the famine was in its worst stage, literally mowing down the people. Their corpses were to be met everywhere, like dead thrushes after a great frost and snow, in the drains by the roadside, along the fences, in the fields, in fact, in the most unexpected places, for they went about in hundreds seeking food, and as they went, they fell, never to rise again, their faces as pale and thin as the face of the moon when she first comes in. Young as I was then, what I saw every day taking place all around me made me as thoughtful as a full-grown person.

As young as I was, I came to the conclusion that there were two distinct races of people in my native parish at the time of the famine. One race I thought was hardier than the other, and I cling to this opinion still. The fair-haired, fair-skinned, freckled people were a terrible sight to see. Their legs swelled, and the skin broke around the calf of the leg and fell off their shins, and from the fringes of skin there hung drops of yellow-green water which trickled down their raw shins, a dreadful sight to see. These fair-skinned people perished about the fourth day of the fasting, but of course, long before death they were worn to shadows, while I have never seen the dark-haired, swarthy people in such a state. The dark people fought a terrible battle for life. They died about the sixth day of the fasting, and some even lived for nine days, for I often listened to my parents and others discussing this matter.

When Gordon determined to start a colony in Bunowen, it was then a village of thirty-three houses. Twenty-three of these have been obliterated and have vanished, and those who lived in them have been scattered by the four winds of heaven, but as I write I see them clearly with the eyes of my mind. I see those vanished houses and the ground on which they once stood; I see the faces and forms of the people who dwelt in them, and I hear the sonorous, loud-toned voice of one of the men as clearly as when he sang the grand old Irish love songs, a sad memory of the days that are gone forever.

Beside the house in Bunowen where the priest then lived, there is a bend towards the South in the road to Louisburgh, and from that bend there ran a boreen towards the East which met the road leading from Long Street, Louisburgh, through the eastern portion of Bunowen, and on through Balure Legan to Old Head. On that end of the boreen, at the bend of the road beside the priest's house, there stood for ages five houses inhabited by a little sept of the O'Grady's, who were nicknamed the Froukaghs, or Frenchmen, in consequence of their being fighters in the Galvanagh army. The old patriarch of the little sept, Tom Grady, was the grandest old peasant I have ever seen, and it was in his warm, bright kitchen, when I was a child, that I learned to love my native land, its glorious songs and legends, for Tom Grady every night in the year harboured some wandering, harmless beggar-man or two, who were brimming over with songs and legendary lore, and we little chaps gloried in listening to these old men. His home, I dare say, was one of the oldest stone houses in the West, for any person who knew the manners and customs of the peasantry could read its age without asking a question. When an Irish peasant built his cot and went to reside in it, on the first St. Brigid's eve that came on, he made a small cross of timber or of straw and tacked it on the screw on the inside of the house, always on the right hand side as you entered the room, and on every St. Brigid's eve, from one generation to the next, a cross was tacked on the roof. All you needed to do to calculate the age of the house was to count the crosses tacked on the roof of Tom Grady's house.

These five houses of the O'Grady's were the vineyard of Naboth for which Gordon longed, in order to turn them into a "jumper" colony close to the parish priest's cheek. Potter, the Louisburgh parson, and Gordon laid the matter before Lord Sligo who very kindly evicted the grand little sept and handed over their once happy homes to Gordon. The Gradys were banished forever from their ancestral homes and soon they became extinct, for they were scattered like chaff before the wind. These were the grand O'Gradys who at all times held open their friendly doors where weary travellers loved to call at this resting place of the wandering minstrel, this asylum of the forlorn mendicant; now there is not even a stone to mark the ground on which these homes once stood.

When the homes of the evicted O'Gradys were filled with converts, the parson and Gordon decided to give them a beef dinner on the first Friday of their installation, an event at which all the elders of the church were to preside, but when the savoury food was served, not one of the converts would touch it, not even if they were to be shot from a cannon's mouth. However, one man who was nicknamed Tony Mirrish, a poor, starved creature, longed for the meat, and I suppose that he also wished to show the holy man that he was a true convert. He ate the beef to repletion, but he paid the penalty, for there was an eye that never sleeps looking out from Heaven at the terrible example he was showing his almost famished, abstemious comrades.

Before an hour passed, Mirrish swelled to the bursting point, and what do you suppose he did? He began calling loudly in his native language for the priest, and the parson, Gordon, and the rest of them were astounded. "Ah, ma curp agus monam urth!" he shouted to his pale, careworn wife, "run for the priest, run, a clyra, if ever you ran and bring me the priest!" She sprang up, casting her conversion to the winds, and ran to Father Myles who lived just beside them, and casting herself at his saintly feet, she told him all with tears streaming down her cheeks.

Father Myles was too prudent to be caught in a trap, for he knew that if he went by himself the parson, Gordon and the strange preacher might murder him. He sent for two of his neighbours, men who during the famine acted the part of Tobias, the elder, in burying the dead. They gathered the men of the village who accompanied the priest to the sick man's house where they thrashed the parson, Gordon and Company, and trampled them in the gutter. The priest anointed the unfortunate man who lingered in great agony for about a week, for in going and returning from a hedge school which was held in the town we little chaps used to stand at the bend of the road, listening to his dreadful shouts.

When Tony Mirrish died, there was another pitched battle for his corpse, for all the forces of the new Jerusalem of Bunlehinch were gathered in order to have the grave of a convert to show to visiting officials. When they reached the bend in the road where the boreen met it and where there was always a large flash of water, Father Myles and the villagers met them. There the battle began, and soon the parson, Gordon and the preacher lay wounded and wallowing in the ensanguined little, shallow lake. It was like a struggle of the angels of light and the angels of darkness over which would possess an immortal soul, but, as usual, the angels of light triumphed and the villagers bore the coffin to Carramore Strand and buried it in the now obliterated sandbanks. Why there was no prosecution I often wondered, but I dare say that no petty sessions were held in Louisburgh in those days, or if they were, I never heard of it, although there was another kind of court held there once a month.

This court, presided over by a paid official called a Seneschal, was called a Brehon Court, and it came down to us from pagan times. The Seneschal was something like an R.M. of our times, but I think his salary came out of the county rates. His power was limited, for in all cases, no matter how trivial, he had to have a jury of twelve men to assist him. The Brehon Court was held in a room on the ground floor of Grandy O'Donnell's house and existed until about the year 1850. I believe this was the last of its kind held in Connacht. The Seneschal, whose name was John Burke, was a fine man in the prime of life. He was also coroner of the district and lived in the parish of Bekan. When we got an hour to play, we went into the court in order to see the Brehons in full session, and there we often stood looking at them with astonishment like Brennus and his Gauls gazing at the senator of ancient Rome, and in our juvenile opinion these men seemed to conduct their deliberations with much dignity and decorum, for never was there a sentence of death pronounced in that ancient, merciful court.

About the year 1853 all the bogus converts fled from the colonies like rats from a ship on fire, and everyone of them returned to the faith of their fathers, ungrateful converts after all the stirabout or bruchawn they had consumed for seven or eight years on the saintly Irish Church Mission! Then it was revealed that the Mission had exhausted its funds, nor was this to be wondered at, for its adherents had squandered millions in feeding hypocrites and in building colonies, towns, in fact, in every parish along the shores of the wild Atlantic from Achill to Dingle, and in hundreds of other places too, and now they had nothing to show for this enormous outlay save hundreds of ruined, empty buildings whose smokeless chimneys became the breeding grounds of flocks of jackdaws.

In the days of his old age, Gordon got his mittimus, for

the work was a failure, and he was given to understand that his services were no longer needed. Then the sensation of that age set in, for the news spread that Gordon would be at Mass next Sunday and would read his recantation, and all the people were overjoyed. When Sunday came around, and Father Michael Curley, who had succeeded the late Father Sheridan, had finished Mass, Gordon came out of the sacristy, stood on the altar, and read his recantation, following which he delivered a very penitential address.

There stood Hugh Gordon in his old age, erect, tall and gray, a man of grand physique. As I, a small chap, gazed at him, my heart bled to see his humiliating, forlorn condition, and I thought that those who by their greed and folly had caused his fall would have much to answer for. He was the grandest old man I ever beheld. The priest announced that there would be a collection held in that church and in the church of Gowlawn that day week, and the people took it up with much enthusiasm so that when the next Sunday came, both collections amounted to forty-six pounds, which was handed over to Gordon.

When this sum was spent, he was too proud to beg, so he walked on to Westport and entered the Workhouse where he died in a short time. His sad story shows us two things clearly; first, how cautious and careful men ought to be who are chosen to arbitrate in a dispute between neighbours, before they give a final decision, for if the trivial dispute I have recorded had been wisely handled, Gordon might have lived and died what he was in the beginning, a most respectable and very much respected man. His story also shows what dreadful results may follow from the act of a man who by foul means grasps the little field or vineyard of his neighbour, Naboth.

THE ADVENTURES OF
FORANAN O'FERGUS, THE PHYSICIAN

About the beginning of the seventeenth century there dwelt near the village of Borus a man named Foranan O'Fergus, and the little green toonagh or hillock where he lived, located between Borus and Forigil at the foot of the brown hill of Cuck-a-Kishawn, is called even to this day Auththie Foranan, which means the place of Foranan's house; surely O'Fergus must have left his footprints deeply imprinted on the sands of time when the name of the glen in which he lived is handed down to posterity.

This old man was a medical doctor, for the O'Ferguses were for at least five hundred years the acknowledged hereditary physicians of the Western Owls of the O'Malleys. They were all skilled leeches, for they had to undergo a rigid course of training from their fathers who kept a careful record of all the cures each effected during his lifetime, together with notes of how he treated the various cases of different maladies which came to his notice and which he cured, as well as the peculiar cases in which he was not able to effect a cure. These valuable records were written by hand, generally in Irish, and sometimes in Latin, for the art of printing was not in vogue in those days in the far West. The reader can see from the foregoing that the O'Ferguses weren't quacks, but were learned physicians. They were a small tribe or clan and don't seem to have been a prolific race, but they were far-famed, the males for their fine, masculine physique and florid complexions, the females for their beauty and feminine grace and winsome ways.

In the days I write about, the great valley which environs the little town of Louisburgh in West Mayo was all covered by a primeval forest so dense that if a man mounted a tree branch at Fairy Hill on the seashore at Bunowen, he could travel from branch to branch without touching the ground until he reached Glan Bawn, a distance of at least six miles. The grandparents of the present writer saw it in the state I have described when they were children. How it was denuded of its timber in such a short period is astonishing to me, but it can be accounted for by the fact that the invaders, the Brownes, the Binghams and the Palmers, cut down the woods in which the rightful owners, whom they called Rapparees, were concealed, for well they knew their lives were in danger until the woods were cut down.

On a certain day in summer, Foranan O'Fergus received two urgent calls, one from the bleak, storm-swept village of Cloonthic, some distance West of the charming vale of Cloonlara, where a man lay dangerously sick, and the other to visit three young men who lived in a little ravine called Dereen-an-Albanagh, on the banks of Killary Bay, about a mile or two distant from its mouth, and who had been greviously wounded in a very peculiar manner. When Foranan had breakfast, he began to prepare to set out. He took down his Bireath or Baret cap, a Celtic headgear which resembled a Turkish turban; as usual he blessed himself by making the sign of the cross before he placed the cap on his head.

66

Next he took down his skean dhu which hung in its scabbard on the wall of his bedchamber and he hung it on his right hip, for in those days no man dared go abroad without it for the woods were infested with wild hogs, wolves, and enormous wildcats. He put on his kothamore or Celtic cloak, the most becoming garment I have ever seen on the back of a tall, well-shaped man. I dare say this garment is now extinct, for I haven't seen one in over sixty years. O'Fergus next caught hold of his Kleagh alpeen or alpinstock, a pole about six feet long, sharpened on one end, which our ancestors used for hill climbing. He called to his side Flann, his great wolfhound, blue-coloured, coarse-haired and brown-eyed. He was thoroughly equipped for the journey as he crossed his threshhold and disappeared through the wild woods. His wife, who had De Danann blood in her veins and who retained some of their superstititions, caught a live coal with the tongs and cast it on the floor in a peculiar manner. If the tongs when cast opened wide it boded good, but if the tongs did not open to the full extent, this boded evil. She cast the coal skillfully, but the tongs didn't open, and her heart sank within her, for well she knew by the unlucky omen that the partner of her joys and sorrows would encounter many dangers before she clasped him again to her white, throbbing bosom.

Foranan held on his way towards the West and soon issued from the woods at Tully. He crossed the river with his faithful Flann by his side, climbed Run-na-hallya and traversed the great moor called Ru-na-goppal; soon he reached Furmoyle, once the happy hunting ground of the far-famed Fena of Erin. He continued on through Carra-an-Iska and the charming vale of Cloonlara, and soon reached Cloonthie where he entered the humble home of Roger O'Toole who lay on his death bed. When he entered the dark, rude cabin, many of the old men of the village followed him, for they wished to salute their hereditary physician.

The doctor examined the wounded man, and then turned towards the villagers to ask, "This man must have got a fall from some tremendous height or cliff, so pray tell me, Toby Stanton, how did it happen, for his spine is broken, and he has but three days to live." "Musha, doctor," said Stanton, "he did get a great fall, and it was all his own fault for he would not be advised by us, for although a small man he was always headstrong and contrary, and now this is the end of it and I often told him so, for he would fight with his nails, and yet he was a good neighbour, the c[^]athereen.

"About two months ago," he continued, "O'Toole sent his fine mare grazing on the wild mountains of Mweelrea, and his son went out to see her each Sunday, and she was coming on fine. Last Sunday when the boy went to see her, she was dead in Lugataree on the shore of Doolough, at the foot of the great cliff, cast down by the eagles. There she lay on the broad of her back and with her neck broken, so the son returned weeping and told his father. The father got into a rage and swore he would have it out with the eagles. The next morning he took down his skean dhu and hung it on his hip; next he took a brown flannel quilt which he rolled up and placed under his arm, and he set out for Doolough, some five miles distant from his home. We followed him, for we knew something terrible was going to take place.

"When we reached Glan Cullin on the western shore

68

of the lake, we saw the dead mare in the deep, dark glen of Lugatharee, at the foot of the great cliff. We lay in ambush under the wide, spreading holly trees while O'Toole went on towards the dead animal. He drew his skean and ripped her open as she lay on her back. He removed the entrails and hid them, and then he wrapped the old quilt around him and lay down in the cavity of the carcass. Suddenly a strange thing happened, and the climax came sooner than we had expected, for two great eagles floated down from the cliff and alighted on the carrion. O'Toole stretched forth his right hand and took hold of the leg of one of the eagles above the talons, while with his left hand he caught the other eagle in a similar manner. The sacred monsters arose with a scream and took wing, carrying O'Toole with them, for the brave little Celt held on to them like grim death.

"There was a strong wind blowing which helped them to soar aloft towards their home in the terrible precipice. O'Toole must have realized his terrible position as he hung in the air between heaven and earth, for well he knew they would tear him to pieces or cast him headlong into the dark chasm. When they had raised him a hundred feet in the air, he loosened his grip and fell with a great crash on his back on the soft morass. We rushed towards him, but we found him stark dead, so we cut down some roan saplings which grew among the holly in the glen, and of these we made a rude litter on which we carried him home with much grief. When we reached home, we found to our astonishment that he had life in him and could take a sup, and it was then, doctor, that we sent for you," concluded Stanton. "Well now," said Foranan, "send for your parish priest, Father David

Lyons, to anoint him and prepare him for eternity, for he has only three days to live." "We will send for him, but it's hard to locate him," said Stanton, "for you know he has no house or home of his own, and never had." "I know that," said Foranan.

Father David Lyons was born in the village of Kelladoon, midway between Killary Bay and the present town of Louisburgh. When he was twenty years old, he went to Spain and entered the College of Salamanca where he remained until he was ordained a priest, and then he returned to Ireland to be appointed by the Archbishop of Tuam as parish priest of Kilgeever, his native parish. He never had a curate, for although he was a small man, he possessed more than one man's share of strength and vigour. While he was in Spain he never met a man fit to wrestle him, nor did he ever meet one in Connacht fit to wrestle him either. Until the day of his death he never had a house or home, but went about from village to village, sleeping in the houses of the country people, on some straw in a corner of the kitchen, for he didn't know at what moment he might have to spring up and rush to the mountains for safety, for the priest hunters were abroad in the land in those days. He never accepted dues, save what should go to the bishop; he never had a farthing in his pocket, or in a box or a trunk, for he never had a box or trunk.

He always wore a body coat, vest, and breeches of black frieze, a strong pair of brogues over which he wore a pair of knitted spatters, all of which he got from the people, but although he was dressed in this humble garb, when he took out his stole, and kissed it, and placed it around his neck, he could dry up the Red Sea or bring down Manna from heaven. He lived to be a great age, and he was vigorous to the last. He died in his native village, and he lies slumbering in a nameless grave in Killeen in the charming vale of Cloonlara, where perhaps his slumbers are as serene and tranquil as those of any canon or other dignitary of the church who might leave eight or ten thousand pounds behind him to some worthless relatives who may never offer up a prayer for the repose of the soul of the benefactor who left them the windfall.

Leaving Roger O'Toole to the ministrations of Father David Lyons, Foranan departed and set out for the banks of the Killary, and as the shades of evening were beginning to descend he reached his destination and entered the dark, rude cabin of Ulick Burke whose three stalwart sons were grievously wounded and disfigured, for each of them had lost half a nose. Foranan stood in the cabin, spellbound and appalled. "How in the world did this happen, pray tell me at once," he said. "Oh no, not until you have partaken of some refreshments," answered the old man, "for it is a long and sad story." The old woman got up and handed him a noggin of boiled new milk sweetened with honey, into which was poured two glasses of poteen or iska baha, and when he had taken this strengthening beverage, he sat down to dinner.

At the conclusion of the meal, the oldest son began to relate his sad story. "About a week ago," he said, "I went to bed just after saying the Rosary, and I fell into a tranquil sleep, but about the dead hour of the night a Naugh stood at my bedside." [To enlighten the present-day reader who may not know what a Naugh is, let it be said that it is a friendly kind of ghost of whom the peasantry were not afraid, for the Naugh came to tell the sleeper where he would find a hidden treasure.] "The Naugh stood at my bedside and said to me, 'Go to the lake of Althor which lies beneath the northern bank of the rugged hill of Derrygoriv. There you will see a firm turf-bank, and when you reach the centre of this bank, stretch on your stomach and look beneath you into the lake. There you will see about two feet of the bogdale tree which is embedded in the bog protruding into the water; look closely at it, and then you will see a pot hung by a pothook on it, just as if it hung over a fire. The pot is filled to the cosheen with gold, but around the cosheen you will see coiled an enormous serpent which is nothing more or less than the spirit of the dead miser who hoarded up this gold. Then insert your gaff under the pothooks, lift up the pot and with all speed run towards the stream which divides two townlands; jump across it with the pot, the spell will be broken, and the gold is yours.'

"The Naugh came to my bedside the second and third nights, repeating the same advice, so on the next morning I took a strong gaff with me and set out for the lake. When I reached it, I made for the northern bank and began to investigate in order to locate the pot. Sure enough, I saw it hanging on the beam some six feet below the surface. Then I stretched on my stomach in order to catch hold of the pothooks with the gaff and lift up the pot, and then the serpent looked up at me with her terrible green eyes, and at once I became fascinated and helpless as an infant. Nor could I move hand or foot, but kept looking at it spellbound until it stiffened itself, reached up and deliberately bit off half my nose and disfigured me for life. Then my two other brothers attempted to lift the pot, but each was fascinated and spellbound, so each of them also lost half a nose." "Well," said the doctor, "I am unable to furnish you with new ones; all I can do is to give you some ointment which will soon heal the wounds. Just rub it on like vaseline or Zam Buck, and in a few days you will be all right."

The next morning, Foranan arose early and determined to climb the western brow of the great mountain in order to take a short cut to his home in the East. He didn't need to climb to its apex, but only to the table land beneath the great cone. Even this climb was a task which would have deterred Hannibal in his best days, but the doctor was bound that he would surmount all obstacles and achieve his goal. He caught hold of his kleagh alpeen or climbing pole and began to climb the southern side of the great mountain of Mweelrea which bulges out and overlangs the waters of deep Killary Bay, for he had learned climbing since his earliest youth, and he had a nerve as strong and a step as firm and sure as that of an Alpine Ibex, and as he climbed his ever-faithful Flann kept close beside him. When he had climbed some fifteen hundred feet, he reached the plateau or table land which stretched away from South to North, the whole breadth of the hill, as vast and undulating as an American prairie. He held on his way toward the North.

When he had traversed about two-thirds of the table land, he came to a lake which tradition states is inhabited by a fiend, or by many fiends. This lake is called Lough Cum, or the lake of the hound, and it is supposed to have the most beautiful gravelly shores of any lake in Ireland. Tradition says that if a man stood on the shore and challenged the lake to send up a champion to fight him, the lake would produce a champion. Or if a man called upon the lake to send up a dog to fight his dog, the lake would send up a black hound who would rend his dog.

Foranan did a deed of folly which he had cause to regret until the day of his death, for in order to test the legend, he called on the lake to send up a hound to fight Flann. No sooner had he uttered the words than the great black hound arose out of the lake and the fight began. It lasted from noonday until the sun was fast waning towards the West, and Flann was torn and wounded in many places, and his life was fast ebbing away. Then the lake hound caught him by the throat and sprang into the lake with the wolfhound's thrashing form, never to rise again. Foranan smote his breast, realising that with his inquisitiveness and folly he had lost his ever-faithful friend, a friend who so often hazarded his life in order to save his master, and now he was gone forever, the true and brave Flann.

With despair in his heart, Foranan fled down the deep declivity of the mountain, leaving that lake of demons far above him. He reached the lowlands between Doogan Hill and the little hamlet of Shraugh Rusky, six miles across the level moors from his home. He began to traverse the vast moor which stretches northward from Glankeen and Derryfeach and trends downward towards the villages of Lachta, Shraugh-na-lusid, and Shraugh-na-cliha. When he reached the centre of the moor he encountered a lake, a portion of which was overgrown with tall bulrushes, while the other portion was covered with beautiful white water lilies which glinted and sparkled in the summer evening sunshine. When he drew near the eastern shore of the lake, above which grew a shrubbery of sally, hazel and yew trees, he saw a sight which appalled him, a wild hog running towards him. It was a sow who had just farrowed a litter of young ones, and who had heard his footsteps long before he had seen her, and now he knew his end had come. Oh, if he had Flann, the brave and fearless Flann would rend and tear her to pieces, but Flann was lost through his own fault.

He stood there unarmed and defenseless. It is true he had his knife, but well he knew he was no match for the sow at close quarters, for she would rend him with her horrible tusks. He signed himself with the cross and bade farewell to hope, although he was no craven, but an intrepid, dauntless man. He determined to fight to the death with the weapon he carried. He took hold of his climbing pole with both hands, as you would a spear or lance. It was of wild mountain holly, as firm and hard as iron, and sharp-pointed on one end. When the rabid monster drew near him, open-mouthed, he drove his alpinstock with all his strength and vigour into her mouth and it went through her neck behind the ear. He drew out the weapon suddenly, and the sow's lifeblood gushed forth in torrents from the wounds. She fell with a great splash into the lake below and sank forever, and from that day to ours the lake is called Lough-na-Muicka, or the lake of the pig.

Foranan looked up with gratitude to heaven for his escape from a cruel death by the skin of his teeth, and then resumed his journey. He soon reached Shraugh-na-lusid and crossed the great river which could well be named the little Nile, for from its source beneath the great mountain of Curwock at Sachta it winds its way through fertile plains until it discharges its waters into Clew Bay at Bunowen. When he crossed the river, night had set in, that is, if a midsummer's night should be called night——

"For the sun loves to pause, with so fond a delay,
   That the night only draws a thin veil o'er the day."

However, the witching hour of the night had come, and the evil one was abroad seeking whom he might devour. When Foranan drew near his home, he met a sluggish mountain stream in which there was no ford. All pedestrians passing that way had to leap across the river. Just as the doctor reached the proper spot for jumping, some huge, dark object stood on the opposite bank, barring his progress. Foranan went along the stream until he found another spot where he could jump, but again the great beast confronted him. Again he retreated to the proper place for jumping, but the great beast lurked on the other side. He tried several spots, but always with the same result. Then Foranan knew that this was a fiend who sought to exhaust him in order that he would perish on the bleak moor.

Determined to fight once more for his life, Foranan took off his baret cap and blessed himself. He drew his skean dhu out of its sheath, made the sign of the cross on the blade, and then with the bound of an enraged panther, he sprang across the stream and buried his skean dhu to the hilt in the vitals of the demon. A voice croaked forth from the huge, hairy body, imploring, "Good man, draw out your knife and give another stab." "Oh no," answered Foranan, "one stab is sufficient, for tradition says that if a man draws his knife out of a demon, the fiend will then slay him." He left his skean dhu in the vitals of the demon and turned away. When he knocked at his door and his wife cast it open, she saw that his eyes were closed, and she realised that he had encountered a fiend, so she led him by the hand to a straw armchair beside the fire. From the saltbox which hung on the wall above his head she administered to him three pinches of salt in the name of the Trinity. Her husband opened his eyes, the danger of fainting now being removed.

Foranan remained in bed for two days and nights in order to recuperate, but on the morning of the third day he arose with the dawn in order to take his usual walk in the forest. When he reached an open glade he saw an enormous wolf approaching, limping on three legs. The doctor continued to advance towards the lame animal and when they met in the centre of the glade, the wolf looked up at him and began to whine as if beseeching him to look at the paw which he held out. Stooping down, Foranan examined it and found the central ball or heel greatly inflamed and charged with corruption. He took out his lancet and lanced it so that a vast quantity of matter was discharged. "Now," he said, "my noble animal, come with me to the little rivulet and I will wash your wounded foot."

The wolf followed him, and as the doctor was washing the wound he saw a great thorn embedded in the heel, so he drew this out with his forceps and bound up the wound. "Meet me here each morning for fifteen mornings," he said to the wolf, "and I will wash your wound." For fifteen mornings they met, and on the fifteenth morning Foranan said, "Now, my noble wolf, you are quite healed, and you need not come anymore." They parted, and the doctor did not see the wolf for many months. But when Foranan opened his door early one morning, there sat the wolf on the street, and he presented the doctor with three meel cows, and each cow with a calf.

The wolf departed and was never seen again. The cows thrived well and increased and multiplied; they became such favourites among the peasantry that a proverb was originated which said: "Never buy a meel cow, never sell a meel cow, but never be a day of your life without a meel cow."

DEAF HUGH O'FERGUS AND HIS DESCENDANTS

When Foranan O'Fergus died and was carried up to Paradise, his mantle fell on the shoulders of his only son, Doctor Owen Bawn O'Fergus, who migrated from the foot of the brown mountain of Knock-a-Kilshawn and built his home in the great oak primeval wood of Collacoon, which was then the only wood left standing in the West. The remains of this dark wood exist to this day, and portions of the granite walls of Owen Bawn's house were to be seen almost on the mearing between Collacoon and the little village of Gurthalisheen, adjacent to the present town of Louisburgh; this old ruin was always called "Balla Owen Bawn O'Faries," which means Owen Bawn O'Fergus's wall. This man must have lived a quiet, retiring life, for there is very little about him in the traditions or folklore of the region. All that is recorded is that he had four sons and one daughter, named Una or Winifred O'Fergus, of whom I shall speak further on.

When Owen Bawn's family grew up, three of his sons went on board a smuggling lugger at Old Head and were carried away to France where they entered a monastery, and after an absence of seven years they returned to Ireland on board another lugger and landed at Murrisk. They were then three Augustinian Friars, Father Ned, Father Owen Bawn and Father Owlan O'Fergus. They entered the old Abbey of Murrisk and lived and died there. I could not find the English translation of "Owlan" for my Shanachie was an Irish-speaking man, although he was considered the best Shanachie of his day or since in the Province of Connacht. Under his tutelage I spent nine years, nor do I regret it.

The fourth son was named Hugh, and in the traditions and folklore of the country he is always called "Aoidh Bour," which means deaf Hugh, but whether he was deaf I could not find out. He was the last and greatest doctor of his race. When he had learned all that his father could teach him of medicine, he set out for Scotland and entered the University of Edinburgh where he took his degrees. Then he was appointed a professor in the College where he remained for twelve years, at the end of which time he decided to return to his native land.

Just then his native parish of Kilgeever, which I now call Louisburgh, was about to undergo a drastic change, for the last of the Lords Mayo died, leaving no male issue of his son to succeed him. The title fell into abeyance, and was not revived for a generation or two. The widow of the last Lord Mayo of Tibod-na-Mung's breed, the Burkes, married Edmund Jordan of Old Head. She had a daughter by Lord Mayo who had married a Dublin carpenter named Lambert. Since it was a love match, they were poor. Mrs. Lambert gathered all the records she could put her hands on of the family and estate and sold them and her own claim to the estate, if she had a claim. She sold them for a few pounds to the first Lord Altamount, of Westport, who at once took forcible possession of Lord Mayo's vast property West of Croagh Patrick.

Since the days of Tibod-na-Mung until the death of the last Lord of his race, the Lords Mayo held a country seat at Askalaun, some two miles west of the town of Louis-burgh, where they spent much time each summer. The mansion stood on the very spot on which now stands the home of Mr. Pat Durkan, and some of the flowers of Lord Mayo's garden bloomed annually in Mr. Durkan's garden when I was a lad. In this lodge during the life of the last Lord, there lived a younger scion of the Mayo family who was the rightful heir, and who became a claimant to the title and estate. This Burke was poor and friendless; Browne of Westport, his opponent, was rich and influential, but still it was the evidence of the heredit-ary bailiff of the property which was to decide the law suit. I dare say that the point at issue was Burke's pedigree. Tradition says that when the trial took place, the bailiff thought it wise to stick to the rich man, so he perjured himself in favour of Browne, and Burke was defeated.

A generation later, the son of the first claimant put for-ward his claim to the title and estate, and again it was the bailiff's evidence which was to decide the law suit, but this was the son of the bailiff who had given false evidence in the first case. The bailiff had a full-grown daughter who was a charming peasant girl, and the young claimant of-fered to marry this girl if her father would give straight, honest evidence at the trial, but the bailiff refused. He gave evidence in court in favour of Browne, and when he was asked why he did this, he replied, "Did you want me to make a liar and a perjurer of my father in his grave?" Young Burke lost the property, and the bailiff's daughter lost the chance of becoming Lady Mayo. I had the pleasure of being acquainted with this young lady when I was a young man. She was a grand old Irish matron who was always called Aunt Kitty by her neighbours. She was alive when I left West Mayo.

When Browne took possession of the property, one of the first things he did was to send his bailiffs who seized Owen Bawn's cattle for rent which Owen did not owe him. Whether he owed it to Lord Mayo I do not know. The bailiffs drove the cattle to Cahir-na-Mart, and old Owen followed his stock, lamenting and exclaiming, "Oh, I wish Aoidh Bour could hear about this in Scotland!" He continued repeating it as he went along, and it became a household word ever afterwards in the West, for if two neighbours were scolding, the people would say that Deaf Hugh could hear them in Scotland.

As the bailiffs were descending the northern slope to the hill towards Cahir-na-Mart, they were confronted by a strange gentleman on horseback who said, "You have driven the cattle too hard, you have them almost killed, for they are panting and frothing. To whom do they belong?" "They belong to Owen Bawn O'Fergus of Collacoon," they replied. Then the stranger dismounted and looked around him until he saw a spring trickling from the foot of a green hillock. "Get me a loy and shovel," he said to some of the men who had gathered around him, and they did. At his direction, they dug a well, cleaned it up, and it immediately filled and the stranger gave water to the cattle.

That much-neglected well is the most historic well in the West of Ireland and should be as sacred as a shrine to the people of Westport, for it is the last souvenir of old

81

Cahir-na-Mart now in existence. The strange gentleman who dug the well was Deaf Hugh O'Fergus, who had returned to his native land, and the well bears his name, being to this day called "Tubber Aoidh Bour," which means Deaf Hugh's Well, a name which is familiar to the ears of the inhabitants of Westport, for they have heard it uttered every day since their childhood. Now, as I have given them its history, I hope they will pay more attention to this historic, much neglected, ancient spring, the last landmark of old times, and I'm sure they will look after it, for there is not to be found in Ireland a man who loves his native town and its surroundings more dearly than a Westport man.

When Deaf Hugh gave his father's cattle a drink, he paid what Browne demanded. Then he placed his weeping old father, Owen Bawn, on horseback, and they drove the cattle home to Collacoon where Hugh began to practice his profession. On a certain day he was called to attend a sick person in Askalaun, and after he had attended the man and was on his way home, he turned in to see a friend who lived just beside the lodge in which lived Mr. Burke, the claimant of the Mayo title and estate.

Hugh's friend, Mrs. Durkan, boiled him a posset, the usual midday treat in those days, for there was no such thing as porter or whiskey knocking about in peasants' houses in those days when our ancestors were far more temperate and abstemious than we are. Mr. Burke of the lodge next door had three grown daughters, very beautiful young ladies. On that glorious summer's evening, one of the young ladies was taking in some linen which was spread on the blackthorn shrubbery, and she was singing in Irish one of those grand old Connacht love songs.

"Musha, Dr. Fergus," said Mrs. Durkan, "isn't she the finest singer you ever heard?" The doctor replied, "She is a charming young lady, surely, and she has a charming soprano voice, but wouldn't you be astonished if you heard tomorrow morning that she was dead?" "Oh, the Lord save us, Doctor, what's that you're saying? The cross of Christ between us and all harm!" exclaimed the woman. The doctor returned home, and the first news Mrs. Durkan heard in the morning was that Miss Burke was found dead in her bed. Deaf Hugh wasn't a quack, but a doctor, and he was the last doctor of his race.

I mentioned that Owen Bawn O'Fergus had a daughter named Una or Winifred Fergus, who married the famous smuggler, Shemus Fodda O'Malley, of Carramore. These brave smugglers of the West deserve a word, in passing, for they did more for Ireland during the terrible penal times than any other race or class of Irishmen I know. It was those brave smugglers who kept Ireland supplied with priests for a period of two hundred years, for without the smugglers the country would surely have had no priests. When the Tudors, and those who succeeded them, smashed up the trade which was carried on between the great seaport towns of Ireland and Continental nations, the peasantry along the seashore from Kerry to Donegal took up the business. Every man worth his salt along that coast built ships of about seventy tons, called luggers on account of their rig, and they did a vast trade with France, Spain, Holland, and the Channel Islands.

At that time, no man could enter a school or college in Ireland in order to become a priest, so all the young men of the Midlands who wished to become priests made for the western seashore from which they were quietly carried by the brave smugglers to France and Spain, where they were freely educated and ordained priests. They returned to their native land secretly on board some smuggling craft. These men could never have become priests were it not for the loyal smugglers. When they returned to Ireland, these wonderful priests of the penal times put on the garb of the peasants. They needed to disguise themselves, for there were priest-hunters who got five pounds from the infernal Sir John Bingham of Castlebar for every priest's head they brought him. There he sat, watching and waiting to receive a priest's head like Herod waiting to receive the head of St. John the Baptist from his dancing daughter.

When the young Spanish priests, as the peasantry called them, for generally they were educated at Salamanca, the favourite Alma Mater of the youth of the West, put on their peasant garb, each one took his life in both hands and began to labour among his flock, preaching, teaching and administering the Sacraments without any remuneration or reward. All he asked was food and a bed to sleep on as he went from village to village, for the priests of the penal days never had a home from the day of their ordination until the day they lost their heads or died a natural death. They offered up the Mass in the ravines of the great mountains, the crevices of the hills, and in the caves along the wild shores of the fierce Atlantic.

The history of the brave smugglers and the wonderful priests of the penal times, if written, would be as interesting and as sad as the history of the Catacombs, and the struggles and persecutions of the first Christians in pagan Rome; yet there is no mention of how they kept the lamp of faith burning brightly in Ireland in the penal times mentioned in what is called Irish history. I have read all the histories of Ireland published in English, although one was enough, for from the first to the last, they are a repetition of each other. They trot out the battles of Clontarf and Aughrim, and the Siege of Limerick, although there was not an old man or a callagh in West Mayo some sixty years ago but could tell you about these battles from tradition with far more eloquence and pathos than the writers of these histories. I agree with Mrs. Green who says in her beautiful book, *The Making of Ireland, and Its Undoing*, that a real history of Ireland has never yet been written. After this long digression, I will resume my Shanachus.

I have said that Dr. Owen Bawn had an only daughter, Una, who married the famous smuggler, Shemus Fodda O'Malley, of Carramore. They had seven children, five sons and two daughters. Three of the sons when they were grown went on board their father's great lugger in Carramore. Shemus Fodda raised his two great prow lug sails and his jib, for they never had a top sail, and yet the craft never existed that could beat them to the wind or overtake them when sailing with half-sheet. When all was ready, Shemus Fodda drew in his hawsers and set sail for Spain. Una and many of her relatives ascended the great hill and sat down on its summit from which they watched the lugger as she ran towards the southwest along the coast until she disappeared behind the wild headland of Renvyle.

Shemus Fodda held on towards the southwest. When he reached the terrible Slyne Head, he took in sheet, and lay off towards the Blaskets, West of Kerry, and when his sons came on deck the next morning, the beautiful green hills of Erin were hidden from sight below the horizon. Shemus Fodda had the blood of the old sea kings of the Owls circulating in his veins, so he held on his course and soon reached Spain. His three sons disembarked and entered the hospitable halls of the College of Salamanca, nor did Una O'Fergus see their faces or hear their voices for seven long years. At the end of that period, Shemus Fodda raised his sails once more and sailed to Spain where his three sons came on board the lugger as fully ordained priests, Father Brian, Father John and Father James O'Malley. Then Shemus set sail for Inisfail, and how well it could be said and sung of them:—

> "They came from a land beyond the sea,
>   And now o'er the western main;
>   Set sail in their good ship gallantly
>   From the sunny land of Spain.
>   O, where's the isle we have seen in dreams,
>   Our destined home or grave,
>   Thus sang they as by the morning breeze,
>   They swept the Atlantic wave."

When the time drew near when the ship should arrive off the coast of West Mayo, Una O'Fergus and her relatives climbed to the summit of the hill which overhung their village, gazing wistfully all the day long towards the southwest for their return. One morning there was a strong northeast gale blowing down Clew Bay when they reached the top of the great hill, and they saw the lugger on the tack out to sea from Cromp Island, near the mouth of the Killary, towards Clare Island, and they were overjoyed. Still they became uneasy, for the ship wore all her sails without a reef as she scudded along almost leaning over on her beam-ends, and the white spray was washing high across her bow. When she reached Shivdilla, the most westerly point of Clare Island, she put about and then she lay in on the land tack towards the strand of Carramore.

Una and her friends hurried down the hill, and the villagers ran towards the strand in order to welcome the exiles to their native land. On she came, sometimes raised high on the white crest of a wave, showing her bows and much of her keel. The watchers trembled at the sight, but Shemus Fodda was at the helm, and he knew how to deal with the wind and waves; how to ease the ship and yet keep her going. When he drew near the strand, he shook out the wind, and the blocks and pulleys sang out merrily as the halliards ran through them. The sails were lowered, and the gallant craft swung round to her moorings. A boat was lowered for the landing, and soon the three young priests embraced and kissed their mother. They blessed her as she knelt beside the waves, and they blessed the kneeling crowd, after which they all marched in procession to Shemus's house to partake of a banquet, for Una had a beef killed for the great occasion.

Soon afterwards the Archbishop of Tuam appointed Father Brian as Parish Priest of Achill, and Father John as Parish Priest of Ballinakill in northern Connemara, and he sent Father James with him to be his curate. Nothing is recorded of Father John or Father James in tradition or in folklore, save that they served God and their people faithfully, lived and died there, and lie buried in one grave in the old graveyard of Ballinakill.

Father Brian, however, was the hero of the folklore of the Western Owls during his life and for a generation afterwards. When he was going to start by boat for Achill to take up his duties, the weather became stormy, so he determined to reach his goal by walking around Clew Bay. He took hold of his huge oak camog which was cut in the dark green wood of Collacoon, a stick from which he was never parted until two hours before he died in his sister's house in the village of Feenone, and this stick was all the wealth or property he ever had, for from the day he was ordained in Spain until the day he died, he never had a house or home and he never had a pound, a shilling or a farthing in his possession. All he asked was a bed and food, which he got willingly from the good people of Achill. He knelt and got his parents' blessing, bade fare-well to Carramore, and set out on his journey.

When he reached Aughavale, Father Brian lingered to contemplate the then vast ruin which in its glory stretched down far into the meadows West of the road, a ruin which tradition says was not an Abbey but a great college where men were educated and ordained secular priests in ancient times. As Father Brian turned around to continue his journey, he saw coming towards him what he thought was a gorilla. This was no gorilla but a man, and I shall explain how he came to be in this condition.

Some six years before, there lived in Belclare near Aughavale a young married couple, and the husband was jealous of his wife, who was a pure, good woman. He was always scolding and beating her. One day all the villagers had to gather in order to save the good woman from his fury, for he was beating her and saying horrid things to her. The woman knelt and, raising her eyes to Heaven, she said, "Musha, I leave it all to God Almighty." As the man opened his mouth to abuse her, a devil jumped into his belly, as tradition puts it. The man went mad and ran about the country raging; for six years he never entered a house, never washed his face or clipped his hair or beard which became matted and entangled, and his toes became like the claws of wild animals as he went about arguing with some invisible thing.

"What is wrong with you, my poor man?" asked the grave young priest as the creature approached. "There is a devil in my belly these six years," shouted the man before he fell down in a fit of epilepsy. When the paroxysm exhausted itself, he lay on his back in the road, and the devil struck him dumb. Father Brian placed his walking stick against the fence, put his stole around his neck, opened his breviary and began to read. Then he stooped down and struck the man on the mouth with the end of his stole, saying, "In God's name, speak." "Yes, Father," said the poor man.

"Where do you feel the devil now?" the priest asked. "He is in my left side near my heart," was the reply. The priest struck him with the stole over the heart. "Where do you feel him now?" he asked. "I feel him in my thigh," was the answer, so the priest struck him there. "Where do you feel him now?" he asked for the third time. "He is going out through the top of my great toe," said the man, and the priest saw smoke coming out of the man's toe. "In the name of God, stand before me," commanded the priest, and the devil stood before him.

"It was you who caused this man to be jealous of his wife," said the priest. "It was," replied the devil. "Well," said the priest, "you will never trouble mortal man again, for I conjure and command you in the name of Our Lord and Saviour Jesus Christ to go down to hell, and to stand

89

there on the crown of your head and never leave there until the end of time." As the devil vanished, the priest said to the miserable looking man, "Arise, and go to your parish priest, and repent, and return to your much-wronged wife." The man did as he was ordered, and the couple lived together happily. This may seem a wild, strange story, but it happened in Belclare, as sure as I live. This was Father Brian's first encounter with the devil, but it was not his last.

When Father Brian was far beyond middle age, his mother died, and there was no way of sending him the news of her death, for it was winter and the weather was stormy. On the first night of the wake there was a great gathering of the peasantry, among them being a man named Paddy Malley of Bunowen, nicknamed Bryjun, who was supposed to have the loudest call of any man then alive in Ireland. Some of those at the wake proposed that Bryjun ascend Carramore hill and call down to Father Brian in Achill. Bryjun consented. He ascended the hill through the moonlight night, observing that a mild south wind was blowing. He stood on the summit of the hill and shouted down in Irish, "Father Brian O'Malley, come up here to Coramore, for your mother, Una O'Fergus, is dead." Three times he gave this bellowing call across the waters of Clew Bay. The people who accompanied him to the top of the hill came down laughing at what a fool they had made of him, and the incident was soon forgotten.

Just as the cock began to crow, a very tall, spare, aging man with a great Roman nose walked into the place where the wake was going on. He wore a coarse, high felt hat, a black frieze cothamore, a black frieze coat, vest and breeches, a strong pair of brogues, with a pair of spatters by way of leggings, and he carried a large oak walking stick. All the people at the wake sprang up to salute Father Brian. "Don't stir," he said, "for I'll not shake hands with anyone here until I first shake hands with Bryjun, for it was he called me. I was attending a call in Achill Beg, and when I left the house of the sick person, I heard a call, then another, and then a third, and I knew it was Bryjun calling me, for I recognized his voice. I got into a canoe and crossed the bay, nor did I bring a boatman with me." So Una O'Fergus had her three priests at her funeral after all, and with much solemnity she was buried with her husband in the old Abbey of Murrisk.

The tombstone of Una O'Fergus lies at the foot of the old limestone altar, and the inscription on it asks for a prayer for the soul of James O'Malley and his wife, Winifred O'Fergus. In 1869 I raised that flag and I buried the last of the old packmen of the West, Patrick Aoidh Hugh O'Malley, of Shraugh, with them, for they were his grandparents, and I dare say that flag will never be lifted again, for that sept is almost extinct now in Ireland. Almost beside that tombstone there is another one also at the foot of the altar, which records the death of another James O'Malley, the James O'Malley who once owned the salt pans in Kilsallagh. Both these James O'Malleys were first cousins. The reason I have gone into detail about them is that as time goes on some of the stock who are in America may visit Ireland, and what I have written may be of service to them in locating the tombs of their ancestors among the most ancient flags in the old, ruined Abbey of Murrisk.

THE WONDERFUL WORLD OF
HUGH O'MALLEY

When night set in, the company became hilarious and gradually the noise grew in volume until it was almost intolerable, so one of the grand old men of the West called for silence. "Now," he said, "we have had much dancing and singing, so why not have some stories for variety's sake?" This proposal was received with applause. The old gentleman called on the last of the packmen for a story. As I scanned him closely, I could see that he was built on a large scale, for even in his old age he was at least six feet in stature. His forehead was high and dome-like, and on his left temple there was a large mole; his eyes were large and grey, and his nose was inclined to be aquiline. He drank as much whiskey as any man of his generation; he smoked tobacco and chewed it incessantly; he lost much blood in faction fights, and yet he lived to be one hundred and twelve years old. He was the cutest and keenest man I ever knew until a month before his death when insomnia set in, with the result that the loss of sleep caused his mind to wander and he imagined that all the men he knew in his youth and manhood were around him. He died in a state of innocence and second childhood. Such was Paurick Arida or Hugh O'Malley of Shraugh, the very last of that enterprising, intrepid race of men, the packmen of West Mayo.

"Musha," said Hugh, a benevolent smile playing around the corners of his mouth, "the sorra story I have, but I will give ye a piece of Shanachus, and as I proceed with it, if portions of it be dry and wearisome, some of it may interest you, for you will hear things you never heard before at any rate. I was born and bred in Carramore, which until the great famine was considered to be the largest village in Ireland, for it stretched from the great strand along the high road all the way to the mearing of Askilaun, and it also ran down the declivity towards Louisburgh until it met the stream which divides it from Cahir. Had a stranger lodged in a house there, he would not dare to leave it without a guide, for he would be unable to find the house on his return, so large was the village and so similar the houses in construction.

"In those days Carramore and Cahir belonged to an old gentleman named French who lived in the old feudal castle which stood on a rock in the lake of Carramore, a lake which was drained in 1847. Since the name of French is rare in West Mayo, I daresay Mr. French must have been a Galway man who was driven from his inheritance by the inhuman Cromwell and got this fodeen in exchange for it from the Commissioners of Athlone, for history states that they often did such things. However that be, Mr. French was cheated out of his holdings some years afterwards by a roguish attorney named Owen Cressagh O'Malley, of Belclare. This Owen Cressagh also cheated an old gentleman named Gibbons out of his castle and little estate in Kilmeena; the castle was called Cishlan Loff or Castle Laffey. The scoundrel, Owen Cressagh, also got possession of Clare Island by some law process or other. When Owen's son, Sir Samuel O'Malley, grew up and learned that his mother wasn't a lady, he shot her. She was the daughter of a Dublin feather merchant named Reilly. When Sir Samuel's sons grew up, one of them shot the other, and in his old age Sir Samuel lost all the estates his father had acquired by perjury and fraud.

93

"When I was just ten years old, on a certain day in springtime my father had a mehal or gang of men sowing potatoes. My mother had begun to prepare the men's dinner, and as she stood on the kitchen table to cut down some bacon hanging above, she suddenly fell off and died of heart failure. I ran to the field and told my father, and all the men ran to the house with much uproar and confusion. My mother was a McNamara from the far West. In the late evening her mother, accompanied by her two other married daughters, arrived, and their grief and lamentation were terrible to witness. There was a roofless barn attached to our dwelling, and when night set in the Banshee began to wail in the ruined barn. My grandmother and my two aunts got up from beside the corpse of my mother, went out to the barn, sat down beside the Banshee and began to wail with her. As the wail of the three women arose on the night air and mingled with the wail of the spirit, it was something weird to listen to, nor did they cease this sound until the cocks began to crow.

"When the time of burial arrived, there was a long consultation as to which of the two graveyards they would bury her in, for there were two graveyards then in the parish, namely, Dooya an thompal and Killeen, for although Kilgeever gave its name to the parish, it wasn't used as a cemetery until very recent times. Some families buried their dead in the Abbey of Murrisk, but none in Kilgeever in those days. The vast portion of the peasantry in the far West believed that Dooya an thompal and Killeen were the two most holy and blessed spots in all Ireland on account of the traditions handed down to them by their ancestors.

"In ancient times a vast green plain, or a beach rather,

94

stretched along the seashore from the village of Kinadooya to the mouth of the Killary, a distance of some three or four miles, and tradition states that in summer time this vast, beautiful plain was covered with bees gathering honey from the white, wild clover blossoms. High above the plain in a gorge on the side of the stupendous Mweelrea mountain, there stood a little stone church or oratory, dating back to the earliest Christian times. This little church was roofed with stone on the principle of the arch, like St. Dara's church off the coast of Carna, or that of Ardfert in Kerry. Some distance from the little church there stood four rude stone crosses facing the four cardinal points, in consequence of which the gorge where the little church stood was called by the peasantry 'Maum na gress' or 'cress,' the gorge of the crosses. There it stood, far removed from any human habitation, some fifteen hundred feet above the vast plain; there it had stood since the sixth century, but tradition had forgotten the name of its saintly founder.

"On a certain fine evening in summer time when the peasant girls from the numerous villages which lay at the foot of the great hill climbed towards the gorge in order to milk their cows which congregated there every evening, the little church stood there in solitary grandeur, but when the peasantry arose the next morning, the little church was standing on the green plain at the foot of the hill. There it stands like the House of Loretto, the wonder, the admiration and the pride of the natives who came in haste and amazement to gaze at this phenomenon, or miracle, rather, and the peasantry called the plain around the little church 'Dooya an thompal', or the sandy beach of the church. This is the origin of that blessed graveyard, and surely it isn't to be wondered at that the peasantry of the far West wished to be buried there when their pilgrimage was finished in this vale of tears.

"Midway between the Killary and Louisburgh lies the vale of Cloonlara which cannot be surpassed for its charming pastoral scenery. It is surrounded on all sides by swelling uplands which shelter it from the prevalent storms of the wild Atlantic, and the verdant fields go down to a limpid stream which glides through the centre of the vale. When the river reaches the village of Cloonlara, it is sheltered from the prevalent storms. Here the villagers placed great square boulders at intervals across the shallow ford, across which they laid long lintels, thus forming it into a causeway for pedestrians, and in this way adding much to the embellishment and picturesqueness of the rural scenery. Amid such surroundings there once stood the venerable church of Killeen, and in the ground around it the peasantry of the central portion of the parish of Kilgeever were accustomed to bury their lamented dead.

"This church must have been a place of great sanctity on account of a privilege which it enjoyed, a privilege not enjoyed by any other church in Christendom, nor can I find anything in history to resemble it, save among the Jews who caught hold of the horn of the altar when in danger of their lives. The privilege, as contained in tradition, is that no matter what crime a person has been guilty of, even murder, if he escaped and ran to the church of Killeen and placed one of his fingers in the keyhole of the church door, he would be let go free. Not a trace of this venerable church now remains, and no one knows who the vandals are who carried it away. In the graveyard there stands a Legaun or pillar stone which is some seven or eight feet high. This stone seems to be half Christian, half pagan."

At this stage of his narrative the old packman, Hugh O'Malley, rested and drained his glass before he resumed his shanachus. "When my father was two years a widower, he went down to Castle Laffey in Kilmeena and married the daughter of the Gibbons whom Owen Cressagh cheated out of his estate, and he brought her back to Carramore. She was an angular old maid with a pronounced aquiline nose, and when she looked at me with her terrible, cold, steel-grey eyes, my heart sank within me, for I knew she would soon comb my hair with the tongs or the blackthorn, and from the day she entered the house, I saw that my father only played second fiddle. Some six months afterwards she took me to the door and hit me on the posterior with a kick which planted me on the dung heap, and she ordered me out. Then I realized that I was an orphan and an outcast.

"I knew an uncle in Cahir-na-Mart, but how to reach him was the problem that confronted me, for in those days there was no road from Cahir-na-Mart to the far West. How then did the peasantry of the West reach that town? All the principal villages were located along the seashore, for a vast moor stretched westwards from Kilsallagh to the vale of Cloonlara, a distance of at least eight miles. This vast bog abounded with fens and sloped down from the hills almost to the seashore and was impassable even to pedestrians. So the peasantry when going to Cahir-na-Mart or any other part of Ireland followed the strand which stretched away from the mouth of the Killary on to the Aughany West. They then traversed Aughany and Polgloss, and then had to cross the rugged side of Carramore hill above the cliffs which overhang the bay when they reached the great strand of Carramore.

"It was then a vast green plain some thirty feet higher than it is now, so they followed it and soon reached Bunowen river which was then merely a rivulet, for in modern times it is the drainage of the vast moor and its reclamation which has increased its volume. They forded the river at a spot where now stands an old ruin called Lundy's Lodge. This ford was then almost as important in its own way as the ford of Athlone was in the old times, for it was thronged day and night by pedestrians, horsemen and horses carrying heavy burdens, and it was called 'Augha na goppal,' or the ford of the horses. Once this ford was crossed, the people followed the trail beneath the cliff of Bunowen and traversed the great dourlin of paving stones before climbing the smooth, big, swelling hill of Derrylahan, descending it and passing through a townland called Logadomba.

"Still they followed the trail along the cliffs of Legan and soon they met the bright, smiling little village of Legan which stood on the western slope of Old Head hill. From here they turned East through Old Head's dark wood at a place called 'Leek-an-afrin' or the Mass flag where the priests in penal times offered up Mass amid the mountains. Soon the travellers met Old Head strand which they followed, and then that of Falduff; next they climbed the little cliff and found themselves in Kilsallagh. Through Kilsallagh and Lecanvey they continued, and when they reached Murrisk they met the Slighe or bridle road which the monarchs of Ireland built from Tara to Croagh Patrick for the accommodation of the hundreds of thousands of pilgrims who visited the holy mountain annually. This road took them to Cahir-na-Mart and the Midlands. I have given all of these details about the route in order to show the present generation of the West the road their ancestors had to follow when going eastward, and this was the only highway we had in starting for Derry, nor was there any other road from the West since the days of Parthalonus until comparatively modern times.

"Well, now, when I recovered from the effects of the kick which I received from the virago, I set my face to the East, determined like Jacob to reach my uncle at any cost. I was dressed as a female and had neither cap nor shoes, and I was just twelve years old. I ran along the great, green beach and passed over the Augha na goppal. Always I followed the beaten track, and I never ceased running until I reached Murrisk, where I sat down to rest in the shade of the historic Hawthorn of Murrisk, which is perhaps one of the most interesting trees in Europe. It is far more interesting than the one at Ardmach which carried on a conversation with St. Patrick, which was all it was capable of doing, while the Hawthorn of Murrisk was capable of depriving men of their lives.

"Midway between Westport and Louisburg, a stream spanned by a bridge comes down through the deer park. Beside the bridge on the North side of the road there stood some forty years ago a little, thatched country cottage in which dwelt a brisk, hardy woman named Widow Machree who kept a sheebeen. At the East gable of this cottage there stood the famous Scahagh of Murrisk, the oldest and most terrible white thorn in Ireland. This bush was the terror of the O'Malley chieftains from the time

99

when the Milesians first landed in Ireland, for if any chieftain of their name wronged a person, all that person had to do was to fast three days and nights, then go to the Murrisk hawthorn at midnight, dig three green sods at the East end of the bush, turn them down with the green side underneath, and at that very moment the chieftain fell dead. Strange to say, this hawthorn had no power over a peasant, whether he bore the name of O'Malley or some other name. Perhaps you will laugh and say, 'I wonder was the bush ever put to the test in modern times?' Indeed it was, and it did its work rapidly and effectively as will be seen in the illustration which follows.

"In the early part of the nineteenth century, there lived in the village of Cartoor, a place located on what might be called the southern slope of Croagh Patrick, a man named Owen O'Donnell, who was much-respected and far-famed for his prowess and dexterity with the blackthorn in faction fights. At the same time there lived in Marino an old peninsular veteran named Major O'Malley. On the pattern day of Murrisk in the year 1829 there was to be a pitched battle between the men of the parish of Lecanvey and Murrisk, and the men of the West, that is, of the parish of Kilgeever. There was no quarrel or enmity between them, but they were going to fight for glory.

"When the day came, both armies were drawn up in the order of battle. The men of the West were tall of stature, fair-skinned, fair-haired and freckled, and had the physique of their ancestors, the De Dananns. The men of the East had all the attributes of another race, for they were broad and sturdy, dark-browed men, descended from the Firbolgs, a hardy race who on many a well-fought field delivered blow for blow, and who frequently gave more than they received. The men of the East were led by their impetuous leader, Owen O'Donnell of Cartoor, while the men of the West were led by the veteran leader of the Galvanaghs, Leim Dhu Nicholson of Bunowen. There they faced each other, ready to hazard their lives for the glory of winning a victory. This kind of dangerous amusement was then the order of the day.

"The two generals saluted each other according to the courtesy of war. Then O'Donnell raised the cry high for Murrisk, and Nicholson engaged him in deadly combat. The action turned into a general engagement all along the line so that the cliffs along the steep sides of the blessed Reek echoed with the clashing of sticks and the shrieks of frantic women whose fathers, husbands, brothers and sweethearts were engaged in strife. Many a brave man bit the dust and lay weltering in gore. With Spartan courage, the Murrisk matrons took charge of the ambulance arrangements, carrying the wounded to Tom Polly's public house which the good man turned into an impromptu hospital; the Murrisk young maidens were the hospital nurses who bound up the wounds with tender care. Then they gave each invalid a gill of Mrs. O'Malley's best fire water which was then considered to be the strongest stimulant on earth. This refreshment revived and invigorated the warriors who craved to be led back to battle. 'Let stakes be placed in the ground,' they said, 'and tie us to them so that we may conquer or fall like our ancestors who perished on Ossory's plain.' The young nurses chided their ardour and administered another gill of a liquid called poteen, with the result that the wounded fell asleep, muttering and moaning as they slumbered.

"All this time the battle raged until the sun was sinking towards the West. The men of the East began to waver, for their general was wounded almost beyond recognition, his nose turned towards his left ear, and the loss of his right eye lending a sternness to his appearance. In good order the men of the East retired from the field, and although Nicholson was the master of the occasion, he was heard to exclaim, 'Give me another victory like this one and I am undone!'

"As O'Donnell and his men approached the gap which led from the field, they met Major O'Malley hurrying towards them, for he wished to review his youth by once again beholding a well-contested field. 'Let me in!' cried the Major. 'Not until we have passed out,' said O'Donnell. The Major was a choleric old gentleman, and now he raised his great walking stick and struck at O'Donnell who anticipated him by striking a terrific blow on the Major's ear. The Major fell as if struck by a catapult, and his retainers carried him home. When the Major recovered, he evicted O'Donnell from his holdings. 'Now, O'Donnell, I have my revenge,' said the Major. 'Yes,' said the ruined peasant, 'but it will be short-lived, for I will appeal to the white thorn of Murrisk.'

"O'Donnell fasted for three days and nights, and at the third midnight he went to the bush, dug up the three green sods and turned the green side underneath. Before the sun rose across the hilltops, Major O'Malley was found stark dead in his bed. This event may have been a coincidence, but it is true as I live, and I know too that O'Donnell returned to his home and was never afterwards disturbed."

Paurick Arida or Hugh O'Malley of Shraugh, the last of the packmen of West Mayo, smiled at the company, his large, grey eyes twinkling as he finished the last of the glass of punch and resumed shanachus. "Well," said he, "when I had rested some time in the shade of the Hawthorn of Murrisk, I arose refreshed and resumed the journey towards the home of my uncle in Cahir-na-Mart. When I reached the field of Annagh, I lingered there to examine the graves of the pagan king of Killadangan and his lazy servant Thulera, and the graves of the unfortunate twin sons of William O'Malley. On the shore of the creek of Murrisk, I examined the boulder on which they sharpened their swords and tested their temper before they slew each other, those sons of O'Malley. The boulder is much worn by the friction of the swords which were sharpened there, and the two cuts made by the twin sons as they tested the temper of their sharpened steel are clearly to be seen on the rock to this day.

"What astonishes me most is that the name of the great pagan king is forgotten and buried in oblivion, while the name of his worthless servant is on every peasant's son even to this day, for if a man has a lazy son or a servant, when rebuking them in anger he will cry out, 'Ah, you lazy vagabond, 'tis depending on Thulera to be depending on you!' In years gone by, often have I heard an angry parent scolding his idle son in this manner: 'Ah, you lazy vagabond, when you were a little child nothing would keep you from running every night visiting to Tom Grady's, listening to all the backaghs who used to get lodgings in that establishment, telling about Fin McCool,

Ossin, Diarmuid and Grainne, Cuchulain and Gaul McMorna, and telling about the pooka, the Banshee, and the old buck with the horns. Now, when you are fully grown and able to work, nothing will do you but this reading about Potiphar's wife, Helen of Troy, Calypso, Cleopatra, Catherine of Russia, Queen Bess of England, and that other vagabond of a woman, Dervargil of Ireland, bad luck to them. Faith,' the father would say, 'I wouldn't wonder but you are trying to be coortin', but no, you ugly villain, there is not to be found this day the girleen who would let you put your come-hither on her.'

"It was this sort of scolding which handed down Thulera to posterity while his master was never mentioned. All that tradition knows about him is that his brother was Queen Maeve's first husband, and I dare say that tradition may be true, for any person who reads that wonderful story, 'Tain Bo Cuailgne,' can see that Maeve's first husband was a Murrisk man. The pagan king's palace was a white, wattled edifice which stood in the dark green woods of Killadangan; through a vista between the great oaks and pine trees it commanded a glorious view of the estuary of Clew Bay and its hundreds of fairy islands, while on the northern shore could be seen the cone-shaped hills of Tieranar and the great, dark mountains of Tirawly.

"High above Clew Bay there stood the Sinai of Ireland, the ever-beautiful Croagh Patrick. There it stood, the darling mountain, the pride, the joy, and the glory of the Connacht peasant, and no matter where his lot is cast, whether famishing in Manitoba, or sweltering beneath the sun as he climbs some terrible skyscraper in New York, Chicago or San Francisco, with his hod on his shoulder, he sees with the eyes of his mind the great blue

104

hill on the seashore, the hill on whose summit Patrick talked to the angels. Then the exile sighs and weeps, for alas! he will never more see it, and as the tears run down his furrowed, sunburnt cheeks, they are caught up by angels who hand them in at the gates of heaven. When he goes to sleep after his terrible day of toil and danger, he revisits in his dreams the happy scenes of his childhood and boyhood, but when he awakens, alas! he finds himself an exile.

"Such was the scenery which surrounded the white mansion of the King of Killadangan. He felt so proud of it that he imagined he was lord and master of sea and land, and he said that to Thulera, his servant, on a certain fine evening in summer time. 'Oh, don't mind the sea,' said Thulera. 'But I do and will mind it,' said his master, 'for it shall and must obey me.' 'I am in doubt about it, your majesty,' answered the servant. 'Come down to the creek,' said the king, 'and I will convince you, for I am determined to test the matter once and for ever.'

"The tide was out, so they took two chairs with them and some iska baha, and they placed the two chairs in the centre of the then-dry channel, sat down and began drinking from great horns of the water of life. Each was armed, and the monarch surely was a sight worth seeing, clad as he was in gorgeous, regal robes; on his brow he wore his most precious diadem, and in his hand he held an ivory sceptre adorned and embellished with gold.

" 'Thulera,' said his master, 'I fear I have chosen a bad comrade, for you have the reputation of being the laziest man in all Erin. What say you about how you are going to conduct yourself on this momentous occasion, for should the water disobey me, I am determined to punish

105

its contumacy.' 'Should it be so rash as to resist and disobey your mandate,' said the courtier, 'I shall assist in
repelling and chastising it, even unto death.' 'Very good,'
said the king, 'brace yourself by partaking of a few horns
of iska baha, for the flood tide has set in, and draw your
sword, for the enemy shall not ambush or surprise us.'

"Just then the flood tide began to hurry in around the
little headland of Annagh, and the channel began to fill
and the water approached the king's sandals. He raised his
sceptre and bade the water be gone, but the inexorable
element continued to advance and soon rose above his
sandals. The monarch arose in fury. 'Draw your sword,
Thulera,' he shouted, 'for the enemy is determined to
charge us full tilt,' but to his call there was no response for
Thulera was fast asleep in his chair, oblivious to all that
was taking place around him.

"The monarch had to contend single-handed with the
relentless element which continued to rise and envelope
him, rising above his hips. But, since he came of a race
which fought to the death, he struck the water with his
bright, flashing sword, sending spray into the air to glint
in the summer sunshine. He tried all the devices known to
sword craft, but it availed him nothing as the water rose
above his shoulders. Then he called and besought Monan-
aun to call back the waters, but the outraged deity replied, 'No, in your vanity and pride you have attempted
to deprive me of my prerogative, and those who defy the
gods shall pay with their lives for their temerity.'

"The king sighed and prepared for the inevitable, but
before he died he administered a final stroke to the waters
before he fell back exhausted and expired. Thus ignobly
perished the great King of Killadangan, the last and great-

est of his dynasty, the noble, young monarch who assisted Fergus in punishing the faithless Conor for his perfidy towards the three heroic children of Usnach, for tradition declares that it was his hand that drove the brain ball into the forehead of the deceitful Conor McNessa. When the tide receded, the monarch lay on his back in the centre of the channel, his trusty sword still grasped in his hand, and beside him sat Thulera on his chair as if slumbering. Then the druids, the minstrels, the poets, the shanachies, and the rest of the people came and with pagan pomp and ceremony, they waked and lamented the king and the courtier for nine days and nights, and on the morning of the tenth day they buried them at sunrise in the field of Annagh."

THE TOWN OF WESTPORT

The old packman, Hugh O'Malley, was fatigued by the narration of his lengthy series of tales, so he lay back in the chair and rested. A fair, beautiful peasant girl approached him, carrying a glass of punch in her hand, and as was usual in those days when offering any alcoholic drink, she kissed its brim with her red lips and said, "Your health, Mr. O'Malley," placed the glass before him, and gracefully retired. The old man tasted the drink, cleared his throat, and resumed the narrative of his travels.

"When I found myself in Killadangan, I determined to visit the witch's cave, for I had often heard the old people talking about the witch who lived in it in the old times. She had the reputation of being the most terrible collagh who had ever figured in song or story, for she could transform herself into any beast or bird in whose shape she wished to masquerade. What she did and how she did it, I am not going to tell on this occasion, because I have other subjects to deal with.

"After I had examined the exterior of the cave, I set my face towards the East and followed the old Slighe Fodda which ran through the region of the green, swelling hillocks lying between Killadangan and Cahir-na-Mart. I ran through Belclare, Aughavale, Carranalurgan and Ardmore until I reached the great hill on whose summit now stands that demoralizing institution, the Westport Workhouse. There was then no demesne wall, so I descended the northern slope and found myself in the sraid balla of Cahir-na-Mart, which lay at the foot of the hill along the southern bank of the river. I entered the home of my uncle, Owen O'Malley, who asked who I was. When I told him, he embraced me, and then he lifted up his voice and wept.

"I soon found that the little town consisted of a long street of thatched houses joined together; this street ran westward from where there now stands the ruins of the old Protestant Church until it reached the present Quay of Westport. It was a seaport, for the tide filled the creek twice a day, and it was the principal rendezvous in the West for smugglers, fishermen and packmen. While I lived there, I often saw George Robert Fitzgerald taking away cargoes of smuggled wine, brandy, rum, and leaf tobacco. The Brownes were looking on, but they dare not interfere, for Fitzgerald only wanted an excuse to shoot them. Later on, the Brownes put a barrier across the creek, turning it into a stagnant pool, and this act gave the death blow to the thriving little Celtic village.

"Westport was a soft, easy spot to live in, for the moorland was all around it, and the turf banks lay beyond the river where there now stands that boxlike structure, the so-called Castle of Westport. The ground on which the new town is built was also moorland which abounded in blind, mossy pools, one of which remains to this day and is called pool-a-cappal, because an Augh Iska or lake horse used to rise out of it and graze on its banks, but when the people approached it plunged in again and disappeared in the bottomless pool. There is a prophecy as old as the hills which predicts that sooner or later the pool-a-cappal will inundate and destroy the town of Westport.

"When Browne compelled the inhabitants of the old town to build the new one, he paved all the streets of the new town with large round stones which he took from Inishlyre, but when this had been done, it was found that no traffic could be carried on over these stones. At that time, Browne had twenty or thirty yoke of oxen ploughing the bogs every day, endeavouring to reclaim and fertilize the demesne, so he put the oxen on the streets of Westport and ploughed up the stones. Then he had the great paving stones broken and he macadamized the streets with them, just as they are at present.

"During the eight years I lived with my uncle in Cahir-na-Mart, a packman frequented the house, for my aunt-in-law was his real aunt. He always had two horses carrying his wares, and he was then aged about forty, for he had been some twenty years a packman. He was the famous Tom Lavelle who composed the once-popular song, 'The County Mayo'. One day he asked his aunt to give me some money, saying that he would take me with him and teach me the business. 'I was speaking to his aunt in Dadreen and she has promised me that she will give him a horse,' he said. So my aunt, who was very wealthy, handed him thirty gold guineas, and the next day I bade farewell to old Cahir-na-Mart and set out for Dadreen in the far West."

THE MURDER OF BOYCE EGAN

"Musha," said the old packman, Hugh O'Malley, "the tale I am about to tell deals with two subjects which most engross the youthful minds of the present generation, namely, love and murder. When I set out with the famous Tom Lavelle to learn how to be a packman, we went to Dadreen in the far West where we were welcomed with open arms by my aunt and her husband, William Egan. They were considered the wealthiest peasant couple in either of the two Owls of the O'Malleys, for the word 'barony' was never used in those days, but only the terms Owl Eagther for Burrishoole and Owl Oughter for Murrisk. The Egans had only two in the family, both sons, and surely one of them was the finest young man I have ever seen. He was named Behalagh, or Boyce Egan. When he found I was going to become a packman, he decided to go with us. Alas! that was an evil choice he made, as time revealed.

"We took a supply of stockings and set out for Derry, where we arrive safely. Lavelle took us to the merchant he always dealt with, a very wealthy gentleman named McKenzie who had no family save a fully-grown daughter who when she saw Boyce Egan, fell in love with him, nor did she try to conceal her passion. He repulsed her since she was a Protestant, and no man or woman in the far West had ever yet married a Protestant. She then offered to become a Catholic, but her father objected. The next time we reached Derry, she offered to elope with him, but he wouldn't have her in that way. Her case was a sad one, for she loved him to distraction.

"When we returned home from Derry, the girl Lavelle was engaged to had married in his absence, so he fled the country and went off to Jamaica, so we were left without our guide and mentor, and we decided to give up the business. At that time there lived in the village of Cross a man named Jack Davitt, a packman. He came to us and induced us to go with him to Connemara to buy stockings, and in an evil hour we consented. When we were ready to start for Derry with him, a strange thing happened. A champion wrestler came to the parish and challenged any man in the parish to wrestle him, but if none could be found who was able to throw him, he placed the parish under a tribute, and he had to be given a certain sum of money before he departed. This sort of thing existed in Ireland since the earliest ages, almost down to our time. It was for vanquishing a champion of this sort with the sword that Tubor-na-Lung was created Lord Mayo, and it was for a similar deed that DeCourcey became Lord Kinsale, and also claimed the privilege of wearing his hat in the presence of royalty.

"Well, I wanted to see the wrestling, so I set out from Dadreen for Tooreen where Mass was offered up on Sunday, for there was no church nearer in those days. When Mass was over, the strange bully from Roscommon sprang into a field in which there were many stunted trees. He stripped himself naked above the hips and challenged any man in the parish to wrestle him. Not one man responded to his call, and like another Goliath he began to revile and laugh them to scorn. I was leaning on a fence looking at him. His taunts so enraged me that I sprang into the field and alighted on some loose stones which caused me to twist my ankle. Still I ran towards him while he stood and laughed at me, but before he knew where he was I caught him by the left hip and right shoulder, and I lifted him as easily as I would a child. I swung him around, and in doing so I broke his thigh against a stunted ash tree. The roar he gave could be heard a mile off, but in fact he was the weakest man I ever handled. There was much cheering, but it's little I heeded it, for my ankle was throbbing painfully.

"I had to rest for three weeks, and the two Jack Davitts and Boyce Egan set out for Derry without me. When they drew near Derry, old Davitt proposed they should take some food. The food which we carried with us will astonish the refined present-day people. It was called Busthaun, and this is the way it was made: when the women made a churning, they kneaded the fresh, unsalted butter and oatmeal together and then formed it into balls as large as footballs. We carried these balls with us on the journey. Our ancestors maintained it was the most substantial and wholesome food on earth, and I do believe it was. The two Davitts and Boyce Egan went into a field and old Davitt spread a cloth on the grass, and so they sat down to dinner. Each man drew his skean dhu, or Irish dagger, out of its scabbard on the hip, and began to help himself from the great ball of Busthaun.

"When they were almost finished eating, old Davitt

gathered up a handful of crumbs and with all his strength cast them into the eyes of Boyce Egan, blinding him. Then he drove his skean dhu to the hilt into his heart. Boyce, who was one of the strongest young men in Connacht, caught old Davitt, smashed him with his fist and knelt on his breast. Just as Boyce was about to stab old Davitt, young Davitt came from behind and drove his skean dhu into Boyce's back. With the daggers of his murderers driven deep into his body, Boyce Egan died, a young man who was said to be the finest and most beautiful man in all Ireland.

"Old Davitt took off the murdered man's shoes with the silver buckles and put them on his own feet, and then he took all his money. The two Davitts placed the corpse in a dry drain which was arched over by briars, and they started for Derry, taking the dead man's horse and load with them. When they reached Derry, Miss McKenzie asked old Davitt, 'Where is Boyce Egan, for I see you have his horse?' 'He is not well,' said Davitt, 'so he asked me to take it along with me.' 'How is it I see you wearing his shoes with the silver buckles?' she asked. 'My own were not the best, so he lent these to me,' he said, 'but he didn't forget sending you the two balls of yarn he promised you for the stockings.' She seemed satisfied with his explanation. When the Davitts disposed of their goods they sold the dead man's horse on the way home, and when they reached there they circulated the news that Boyce Egan got married in Derry and remained there.

"About a month afterwards old Davitt asked me to go with him to Connemara to buy stockings. I consented because I longed to see my cousin and comrade, Boyce Egan. We crossed the Killary and were bound for the fair of Dooneen. Halfway between Tully and Letterfrack, he asked me into a field which was surrounded by whin bushes. I agreed, and as usual he took out the Busthaun, spread a cloth on the grass and drew his skean dhu, but somehow I felt uneasy, nor could I eat any of the food.

"I got up and walked towards the fence, and as I looked along the road we had come by, I saw three men coming towards me at a great pace. They had their sticks on their shoulders and their body coats thrown across them. When they drew near, I recognized them. Two of them were brothers named Durkan of Askalaun, and the other was a man of gigantic stature named O'Malley of Glankeen. All three were yeomen. 'Where are you going in such haste?' I asked. 'Didn't you hear?' they said. 'What would I hear?' I replied. 'Jack Davitt and his nephew killed your cousin, Boyce Egan, about six weeks ago near Derry, and we are looking for them.' 'Keep quiet,' I replied. 'Old Davitt is in the field here. I will go down and spring on him, and then you jump in to my assistance.'

"I walked back into the field. 'Who were you talking to?' asked old Davitt. 'Three strangers like ourselves who are going to Dooneen,' I replied. 'Sit down, man, and take some food,' he said. I pretended to do so, but I sprang upon him, caught his two wrists and raised his arms in the air. He fell back, and I placed my knees on his breast. The three men rushed in to subdue him. We took the skean dhu out of his hand, bound him with ropes, and recrossed the Killary with him. The yeomen took him to Westport and handed him over to the terrible Denis Browne, better known as Soap the Rope, who forwarded him to Derry. He was tried there at the next assizes and was later hanged on the very spot where he committed

114

the murder. But no trace could be found of his accomplice, the nephew.

"About six months afterwards, some children were herding cows on the brow of a cliff in the village of Dooaughtry when they saw small slates of shingle being cast from the base of the cliff to skim upon the smooth surface of the sea. Since they often did this themselves, they knew it was some person who was doing it. They told their parents who were aware that there was a cave in the cliff and who guessed that young Davitt was concealed there. They sent word to Boyce Egan's relatives, who gathered in great numbers. They went in by boat and captured young Davitt in the cave. He was handed over to Denis Browne, and was afterwards hanged in Derry.

"The ends of justice were served, but Miss McKenzie was inconsolable and pined for her dead love. She composed a lament for her lover which I used to sing in the old days." The company insisted that the old packman sing it once more, so he sang them the lament of Rebecca McKenzie for Boyce Egan:

> Oh, once I loved a noble youth
> Whose face was fair and bright to see,
> But since he died, in very truth
> This world is all a blank to me.
>
> For now he's gone, alas, from me
> Beyond that dark, mysterious bourne,
> Oh, never more his face I'll see,
> And I am left to weep and mourn.

I'd climb with thee the mountains high,
I'd brave with thee the raging main,
Nor would I even breathe a sigh
Lest that one sigh would cause thee pain.

I'd fly with thee to torrid climes,
I'd tread with thee their burning sands,
Thy voice to me were sweet as chimes
Of joy bells in my native land.

I'd live with thee in deserts bare,
Or in a rude cabin by the sea,
Nor would my heart feel pain or care
When thou wert there and I with thee.

Oh, leave me in a darksome cave
Where summer sunbeams never shine,
Nor fragrant flowers nor shrubs shall wave
Above this broken heart of mine.

But should we meet beyond the grave
In realms of everlasting bliss,
The only wish my heart doth crave
Is to lay upon thy brow one kiss.

Miss McKenzie pined away rapidly and died when the autumn leaves were falling, but before she died she became a Catholic, for she wished that no impediment should stand between herself and her beloved in the world beyond. Although the lovers were cruelly parted in this life by the daggers of the dastardly murderers, they sleep side by side in a fine tomb in the Catholic Cemetery of Derry.

DOONAL MERGEACH,
THE BARD OF WEST MAYO

With much interest, mingled with regret, I have read the article by Professor O'Malley which appeared in a recent issue of *The Mayo News*. Last June I had the honour and pleasure of being introduced to him by a mutual friend, the learned, energetic Father John O'Reilly, and was exceedingly charmed by the mild, unaffected, unassuming manner of the distinguished young gentleman. I was sorry to learn that his late visit to the land of the West in which I was born and bred hasn't been a success. Had he gone there some fifty years ago, believe me, he would have a different story to tell.

Surely the people of the West must have deteriorated terribly since I left, for when I left the West of Mayo some forty years ago, there were hundreds of old men and middle-aged men there who were brimful of songs and traditional story. Now it appears that these fine old Irish songs and interesting old legends are forgotten, and nothing remains save the remeshas of Shaun McNamara, Paddy na Stack O'Toole, and Leim Kirby of Askalaun. They were the last remnant of that terrible class of men who have figured conspicuously in ancient and modern Irish history and tradition, the satirical poetasters, who imagined they were poets. Their inspiration came from the belly, for if you gave them your sweetest bite or last morsel they would exalt you and place you on a high pedestal, but if you refused and didn't give it, they leveled you in the dust and set the world laughing at you. When I was a child in the great famine time, I saw these three satiric poets going about from door to door, and although

I was then only seven years old, I could this day describe them, how they looked, and how they were clad. They received scant courtesy, so they perished and were swept away by the famine.

In the days of Michael Sweeney, there were two real Irish poets in Clare Island. One of them was a match for Sweeney in every way as a poet; his name was Shemus Dhu O'Kerrigan. The other Clare Island man was named Nicholas Doogan, but yet West Mayo never produced a real Irish bard, save one, whose name was Doonal M. McNamara, and it failed the professor or his favourite Shanachee and historian Pat Burke, of Devlin, to find out who Doonal was.

Doonal was the son of Brian McNamara who lived in the village of Caraniska, a townland some three miles west of Louisburgh, and old Brian was the richest man in his day in the parish of Kilgeever. When his son Doonal grew up, he was supposed to be the finest young man, not alone in Connacht but in all Ireland, and he was so fair-skinned and so freckled (for freckles at all times in Ireland were considered beautiful), that his friends from pride called him "Doonal Mergeach," that is, Daniel the rusty.

There lived at the same time in Kilsallagh, a village some three miles East of Louisburgh, a man named James O'Malley. He was always called "Shemus ui Thigue Bawn," that is, James, the son of white or fair Thady O'Malley. This James O'Malley owned great salt pans in Kilsallagh, and it was he who cut away that now worthless strip of land which runs along the cliff from the schoolhouse of Kilsallagh to Lecanvey, for it was there he had his turf banks. This man was considered the richest

man of his time in the two Owls of the O'Malleys, and
he had no children save a daughter then aged fourteen.
Brian McNamara and James O'Malley put their heads
together and made a match between Doonal and Rosheen
O'Malley, who was in fact only a child. Doonal didn't
want her at any cost, for he was paying his addresses,
with much success, to a Miss Fergus, of Mullagh. The
Fergus girls were famous for driving poets into exile.

At length Doonal had to give in to his father's wishes
and get married to little Rosheen O'Malley, but his heart
was in Miss Fergus's keeping. When he had been married
about six months and was living with the O'Malleys, one
night when James O'Malley and his wife were sleeping
in the outshot of their kitchen, the daughter came down
from the room carrying her clothes in her arms, for
tradition states that she was so young she was unable to
dress herself without assistance. "Where are you going?"
asked her mother. "Faith," said the daughter, "I was
afraid in the room by myself." "Where is Doonal?" said
the mother. "When ye go to bed," replied the daughter,
"Doonal goes out every night through the window and
doesn't return until the second round of cock-crow."

The mother got up and dressed herself. "Saddle one of
the horses," she said to one of the servant boys, and he
did so. "Now sit in the saddle," she said to him, and he
did so. The mother sat behind the boy on the horse.
"Now," she said, "drive on to Mullagh." It wasn't far
distant, and when they reached there, Mrs. O'Malley
tapped at the door of Mr. Fergus. "Are you there,
Daniel?" she called. "Yes, ma'am," he replied. "Well, if
you are done there, come home," she said. Doonal came
out. "I am very sorry to bring you out on such a jour-

ney," he said to her, "but I promise you while there is life in your body you will never have to take such a journey again."

Then Doonal Mergeach set his face towards the South, and he never halted until he reached Crataito in County Clare, and he never returned to West Mayo. While at home he wasn't a poet, but when he became an exile it was then the Muses began to smile upon him. He took up the lyre and began to sing, or rather, to weep. When he composed a song, he transmitted it to some friends in the West, and his songs were considered masterpieces by the then clever men who dwelt in the West, and they were sung all over West Mayo for many generations. It grieves me to learn that Professor O'Malley met with only one of them for they were many. Often I heard my father and other men sing them, and when I left West Mayo, there was a man in Louisburgh called Thomaseen Meelan who used to sing them to perfection.

When Doonal's deserted wife grew to be a full woman, a man named O'Donnell from Ballacroy came with many of his clan at night by boat to Kilsallagh and took her away with them. This kind of thing was called "foudagh," and it was quite common in those days. Afterwards, O'Donnell migrated from Ballacroy to Polgloss where some of his descendants lived until I left West Mayo. I dare say they are now extinct. When Professor O'Malley next calls to see his great Shanachee, Mr. Burke of Devlin, I hope he may be able to tell him who Doonal Mergeach was, but then the Professor might say it is some of Mr. Berry's fiction!

PART TWO

TALES OF CONNEMARA

It was evident that the old smuggler, George O'Malley, was in bad form for story telling, for the poor, homeless old seadog had walked all the way from his native place, Achill, to be present at Grandy O'Donnell's wake, but he pulled himself together and began his shanachus. "Now," said he, "as the incidents I am about to relate took place in Connemara, a wild region, which few if any of the present company have ever visited, perhaps a description of it would not be out of place, although I would have you understand that this is applicable to Connemara as it was in 1798, and in a few remote portions of it down to a more recent time.

"Should you take a good map of Ireland, such as can be seen in the National Schools, and look at West Galway, you will see a bay depicted there named Kilkieran Bay, which runs straight to the North through the mountains to a place called Inver, where the present Earl Dudley has a sporting lodge on a small island in Lough Inver. From there a road runs to the North to a place named Shandilla, made famous by the late Major Lynam as being the spot where the famous Mick McQuaid kept a shop; this place is also now known as Maam Cross, and here there now stands a railway station on the line which connects Galway with Clifden. From this station a road runs north to Maam, then turns left through Maam Valley and Joyce Country to Leenane.

"When you reach there, you may imagine the coast line of the Killary to its mouth; all the vast region to the West of this imaginary line I have drawn is the great barony of Ballynahinch, or the vast territory of Connemara, the home of the exile and the outlaw in the old days. Of course, it is not all the wild region which our ancestors called Iarr Connaghta, but it is the impregnable, inaccessible citadel of the wilds of Iarr Connaghta. Once you reached that region, you were as safe as if you had taken refuge in the moon. There was no road of any kind in this vast region, not even a beaten path. There was no chapel in some of the parishes, no priest's residence, no school of any kind, no post office, no dispensary, no court of justice, no police barrack, for there were no police until 1833; hence there was no law, and everyone did as he pleased. The inhabitants were split up into clans or factions, and the strongest ruled the roost.

"All this vast region is almost totally occupied by ranges of high mountains, notably the Banabola range which is the pride and glory of West Connacht. These mountains start up at Corrib in the East, run straight westward towards the Atlantic, a distance of twenty-four miles, but as they approach the great ocean, they, like trees, begin to dwarf, as if stunted by the incessant storms of the Atlantic. When they meet the sea, they terminate in an amphitheatre of small, heather-clad, picturesque hills, in the arena of which stands the neat, modern town of Clifden.

"Between these ranges there are vast moors or swamps, lakes and sluggish streams, tall bulrushes, and a high, keen-cutting species of swampy sedge; woe to the stranger who would try to pass through here without a guide! The western coast line from the mouth of the Killary to Slyne Head is thickly inhabited. When you have rounded that dangerous headland, the coastline runs straight to the East to Galway, and this stretch is thickly inhabited also, although the vast interior is almost un-inhabited, unexplored, unknown and undeveloped.

"How it was that the refugees found their way through and penetrated this labyrinth of nature is truly astonishing. However, they came in hundreds, and were received by the natives with open arms. The first thing they did was to take native wives, for the Connemara maidens of those days were easily wooed and won, and within a generation or so the result of this union was a race of mortals the most heterogeneous to be met with in Western Europe. There was not a type to be seen among the Caucasian race but its prototype could be found in that strange, wild region, although later the great famine and emigration cleared them out."

When the old man had finished his description of Con-nemara as it was in 1798 and long afterwards, one of the matrons of Cloonbawn came into the corpsehouse to offer up a prayer for the departed. At that time there were many grand old matrons in the little town, but this one far surpassed them in hospitality, for she possessed a great share of what is termed the milk of human kindness. She was the noblest Roman of them all. As she arose from her knees, she looked around her and saw the old, homeless smuggler. "Oh! George O'Malley," she said, "did you come all the way from Achill to old Grandy O'Donnell's wake?" "Yes, Mrs. McGirr, I did," he replied. "Musha, may God reward you!" she said. "Come along, George, and have some refreshment." He got up with alacrity and went with her, for I am quite sure he needed it, and yet I was sorry he left, for I longed to hear more about the wild region he had been describing. Alas, how short-sighted we poor mortals are and how ignorant of the future, for it is little I thought that night that one day I would dwell in that land and lay my bones in some lonely graveyard in which so many of my countrymen lie sleeping the calm, long sleep of, I hope, the just.

As the old man left the room, he promised he would return, and I thought there would be silence once more, but in this I was mistaken, for there were two strange mortals in attendance at the wake. One of them was the ugliest man I ever saw. He had a cast in both eyes, and both eyes were affected by cataracts. His cheeks were all puckered, and he had a terribly snub nose. He was knock-kneed, and his legs slanted out in such a way that his flat fleet were set at least three feet apart. His occupation consisted in carrying the vestment box from one station to another for the priests at station times.

When the priests discarded their clothes, they gave them to this man, so he went about the town in a top silk clerical hat with a very broad brim, which it was said came from a bishop; he also wore a black clerical coat, vest and trousers, and he carried a huge, yellow walking stick. A priest he was to look at, but he lacked the Roman collar. All strangers saluted him at once, however. To do him justice, this distinction he never sought, but as the greeting was so kind, he returned it with the grace and dignity of a Cardinal, and in passing he raised his hand, uttering the familiar salutation, "God bless you, my child." Such was Paudeen Rory O'Toole in his day.

The other man was of a different type, tall and thin, with aquiline features. In those days the police could hand their old uniforms to any person who needed them and had cheek enough to wear them, so this man came in for a large share of them. He always went about the town tricked out in a policeman's rig, forage cap and all, and he sported a thin walking stick with a tassel dangling from it. He sang French and Italian songs, moroya, with the skill and pathos of a Caruso, for which he received many tips from strangers. Such was Gogie Ivers in his day.

"The old smuggler will get a good supper and a few bumpers of punch from Mrs. McGirr," said Gogie. "They will be of little use to him," observed Paudeen. "Why?" asked the other. "Because if you put a tube from here to Loughnamucka, and put one end of it in his mouth, if that lake was a lake of whiskey, he would soak it into him and drain it as dry as the floor of an oven," said Paudeen. "He was never fit to drink with old Paddy Malley of Shraugh," said Gogie, "for the wife of the man that's overboard here tonight, poor Nancy Mulloy, God be good to her, tried them at it. When the smuggler had taken twenty-two tumblers of punch, he fell asleep, so Paddy drank twenty-five, and then he took out his mare, Maura-nee-Ortha, and you would not notice that he had a drop taken." "He was a fool," said O'Toole, "for they say that mare was hard to ride, even by a sober man." "Not when you got in the saddle," said Ivers. "Anyhow, she was the best mare that ever figured West of the Shannon, for she never lost a race."

"That was a queer name she had," said Paudeen. "It was a woman's name," replied Ivers, "for Maura-nee-Ortha means Mary O'Flaherty, and I'll tell you how she got the name. When Paddy Malley's son came home a priest from Portugal, he was sent as a Curate to the parish of Ballinakill in Connemara, and his father gave him a racer. He took lodgings in Tully at the mouth of the

Killary, and in the same village there lived a woman named Maura-nee-Ortha, otherwise Mary Flaherty. One morning in the harvest time, her husband went out to his little field to reap corn, so after his wife had milked the cow, she went out to him and tied the six barths of corn he had cut. 'Festy, agraw,' says she, 'go in to your break-fast, for I am going to the blessed well of Balla beyant Castlebar in the blessed county of Mayo, and when I return in the evening, with the help of God, I'll bind all you have cut while I am away.'

"Then she took her ball of thread and her knitting pins and hurried off, knitting and humming to herself in order to shorten the road, moroya. It was not long until she reached Balla and gave her station. She arrived home quite early in the evening, and tied the corn her husband had cut while she was away. She milked the poor cow-een, and she had a fine pair of socks made, so she became famous as a walker. The young priest was very pleased, so he called the racer after her," said Ivers.

"A man in Caraclagan had a mare," said O'Toole, "and his mare had a foal on Christmas night. 'Take her down to the turf bank,' said he to his sons, 'and drown the foal in the boghole.' They did as he desired, but the mare pulled the foal out again, and this took place three times, so they let the animal live. He was a blue colour and not much to look at. When he was three years old, horse races for a saddle and bridle were held in Tooreen, for there was no Louisburgh in those days. One of the young McDonnells who owned him raced him there. He was in before any of the other horses were halfway home. 'Who owns the brunnach?' asked old Tom Ruttledge of Ballyhip. 'He belongs to me,' said O'Donnell. So Tom

128

Ruttledge bought him for six pounds. This horse won all the great races of his day in the British Isles. He was taken to France and won all before him there, until he had to be cried down as being enchanted. This is no fiction, but a real fact."

THE SMUGGLER'S STORY

George O'Malley, the old smuggler from Achill, pulled his chair closer to the fire and prepared to entertain the company with the tale of his adventures in the wilds of Connemara. "In the summer of 1810," he said, "I discharged a cargo of wine, rum, brandy and tobacco in the Killary. It did not take me long to do so, as I had agents on both sides of the bay who took charge of the cargo. Then I overhauled and tidied the lugger, for it was on her fast sailing and speed our lives depended. One evening as I leaned on the bulwarks watching the men who were scraping the ship's sides above the water line, I was admiring the western range of the Banabola mountains, for they were a wonderful sight decked out in their very best summer holiday vestments of purple, green and yellow. Each peak had on its white helmet which sparkled as the sun shone, and these mountains filled my mind with visions of giants who were determined to repel any invasion from the West. I have mentioned the western range, for the Twelve Pins are divided into two ranges by the valley, or rather gorge, of Glaninagh. This gorge begins at Recess where the railway station stands now, and continues on to the Killary, a distance of fifteen miles.

"One half of this narrow gorge is occupied by the beautiful Lough Inagh, while the other half is one vast moor which slopes gently down to the southern shore of the Killary, and as I looked along this moor I saw a man approaching from the South. He continued on his way and never halted until he stood on a little bluff which jutted into the bay, from which he called out and asked to be taken over. I did not wish to disturb the men who were working, so I got into a boat with my face to the bow, for the distance was so short I did not think it worth while to sit properly on the beam. I paddled gently towards him. As I drew near, he stood some fifty feet above me, with his outline cut clear against the dark blue summer sky, and as he leaned against a long gun, the stock of which rested on the ground, he was surely a man of the grandest physique I have ever seen, for he seemed to be over six feet in height, broad-shouldered, narrow-hipped, and light-limbed.

" 'Did you call out and ask to be taken across the bay?' I said. 'Yes, if you please, sir,' said he. I wheeled the boat around and he stepped in on the stern sheet and sat down on the locker. He took off his hat in order to wipe the perspiration off his brow, and it was then I had a real opportunity of looking at him. He was the straightest, the grandest, the most extraordinary man I ever saw. He seemed not to belong to the species I belonged to, for he was as strange to me as if he had fallen from the planet Mars. He was dark-haired, and the portion of it which his hat covered lay smooth and shining on his beautifully shaped head, while the portion of it below the hat curled up in deep waves which were astonishing to look at. In fact, he had as much hair as would spoil twenty men, yet somehow it became him, and adorned him far better than the diadem of an Emperor. His every movement differed from the movements of the race of men I had been accustomed to.

" 'How far have you come today, sir?' I asked. 'Just thirty miles,' said he, 'straight south from a wild peninsula called Errisanagle, just opposite the dark blue Isles of Aran, a rough, unfrequented swamp which was never intended by nature as a home for man, and yet, it is inhabited by a race of ferocious giants. In all that journey from there to here I have not met or seen one of my own species, nor have I trod on solid ground, for the region I have passed through is one vast, monotonous, swampy wilderness where no sound ever breaks the stillness of this horrid region, save the screams of the startled herons.'

" 'You must be somewhat fatigued, please come on board the lugger and have some refreshment,' I said. 'Not until I know who the man is who invites me,' said he. 'Surely I am not so easily decoyed as that.' 'Well, then, if the name of the one who invites you will dispell your suspicions, my name is George O'Malley, the last of the smugglers, who is very much at your service,' I said. 'And I am Brian McNamara, the last of the Rapparees of the West, for whose head Denis Browne, the tyrant, has offered a bag of British gold,' he said. We embraced each other and went on board the lugger.

" 'Now,' said he, 'I shall remain as long as you wish to keep me, for I have no home on this earth, save the great cave of Benlethry, high up in the cliff of the great mountain which looks down on the grand castle of the Martins, once the stronghold of O'Flaherty of the battle axes, the terror of the invader.' We sat over our punch until deep in the night, for I urged him to become a smuggler and join me. 'I would join you at once, but there is a certain matter which I fear would prevent me,' he said. 'Mention it,' said I, 'and we may find some way out of it.' 'Oh,' said he, 'it is a private matter which only concerns myself and another, so there is no use in going into detail about it.' We retired for the night.

"The next morning a young man came on board, the son of one of my agents. 'Roger, is there anything wrong?' I asked. 'No, sir,' said he, 'only we have a Station in our house today, so my father sent me to ask you to join the priests at dinner, and I hope that Brian will accompany you.' When we had taken some refreshment, we were landed in Derreennasliggan where we set out briskly across the great moor which slopes upwards from Killary to Lough Inagh. We soon reached the great, circular sheet of water, Lough Fee, which lies midway between the Killary and the gap of Kylemore, and as we trod along its banks the air was redolent of honey from the heath bells on which we walked, mingled with the scent of the water lily, the bog-bean, and other acquatic flowers which grew along the shore. Further on, we reached the miniature Chapel of Cearagh, the most diminutive Catholic Church in Ireland, standing on a little hillock in the almost interminable bog.

"Finally, we turned to the right and entered the pass of Kylemore, and soon we were shaking hands with hospitable old Roger Coyne of Powlacoppal. I had known the old parish priest already, and now he introduced me to his two new curates. 'This is Father Edward Vaughan, son to Ned Vaughan, the celebrated Westport smuggler,' he said as he introduced me to a very young, fair-haired priest. Of course I knew his father who grew to be a very wealthy man in Westport, for he was most successful as a smuggler, although he was subjected to much annoyance by the Brownes. He was married to a very fine woman named McCaffrey, whose brother, Father Tom McCaffrey, died as Parish Priest of Louisburgh in 1847 or 1848.

"When Ned Vaughan had sired nine children he left Westport in his lugger, bound for Flushing, but he never returned, and the people thought he was lost. His wife and her brother, Father Tom, sent the oldest boy to college, and after this boy was ordained, he was sent on the mission to Ballinakill. After a year or so, he emigrated to America, and the whole family went with him. One day he was in his Confessional in a church in Portland when an old, feeble man entered. When he knelt, the priest felt a premonition of some sort, so he asked the old man where he came from. 'From Ireland,' said he. 'What part?' asked the priest. 'From Westport, County Mayo,' came the reply. 'Have you got a family?' 'Yes, I have a wife and nine children.' 'Don't mind going to Confession tonight,' said the priest, 'and I will accompany you home in order to make their acquaintance, for I am also a Westport man.'

"The priest went to the home of the man, and there his discovered that this was his emigrated parent, and that the same number of male and female children he had by his real wife, he had the same number by the other woman, and the names were the same. The priest told his mother the story, and when she confronted her husband, the shock was so great that it killed old Ned Vaughan.

"The parish priest now introduced me to his other new curate. 'This is Father Edward O'Malley, lately ordained in Lisbon, son of old Pat Malley of Shraugh, near Louis-burgh,' he said, as he introduced me to a very young priest with jet black hair, brown, lustrous eyes, and a long nose, inclined to be snub. This young priest became the darling of the peasantry as a result of an incident which I shall relate.

"When the road between Westport and Clifden was being built, there was a gang of men blasting in the then obscure village of Leenane, and in tamping a hole an ex-plosion occurred, driving the man who held the drill high in the air. He came down in a sitting position, and there were no bones broken, nor had he any flesh wounds, but the cap of his skull was blown off from the two ears. He could talk and had his senses about him, and he began calling for the priest. The priest, however, was fourteen miles away, behind the great, high mountains of Kyle-more and Salruck.

" 'Don't be uneasy,' said the poor, wounded man, 'for I shall not die until I am anointed, for the Blessed Virgin Mary is standing here at my right hand. I see her with my eyes. Go for the young priest in Tully who has the mare.' Then a man who was far-famed for his swiftness stripped off some of his clothes and his shoes, and he ran by short cuts best known to himself, through rugged hills, across vast moors and swamps, through tall bul-rushes and keen-cutting wild mountain sedge. He breasted the great mountain and sprang from crag to crag with the sure-footed, elastic spring of the wild mountain goat.

"When he reached Tully, he quickly found the priest. 'Hurry on, Father,' he pleaded, 'or you won't catch him

134

alive.' The priest quickly mounted his bright bay mare. 'Now, Maura-nee-Ortha,' said he, 'you won many golden prizes for my father, for you have never been beaten yet in a race; gallop now and win this prize for God.' Maura-nee-Ortha began to gallop. She raced from Tully to Letterfrack, then turned to the left through the wild pass of Kylemore, by the little church of Cearagh, and by the shores of the beautiful Lough Fee. Then she breasted the hill which leads to Clinncroff. She galloped through the evergreen valley and on to Deerynaclogh, and then swung round the Killary.

"When she got to Derrybeg, the people who were gathered around the wounded peasant sent up a great shout, 'The priest, the priest is coming!' 'Do not deceive me,' said the poor fellow. 'The priest is coming!' they shouted. 'We hear Maura-nee-Ortha galloping; she is coming with the speed of the March wind.' Sure enough, she was coming, but she seemed to be a white mare, for she was covered with foam, and her rider was white also, for he was covered with the horse's foam.

"When the priest alighted, all covered with mud and foam, a great shout went up. The priest took out his stole, kissed it and placed it around his neck, donning the sacred emblem which our ancestors believed helped him to remove mountains or conquer all the infernal legions, that emblem which has figured so conspicuously in all our ghost stories and our folklore. The priest put on his stole and anointed the wounded man, who with faltering voice said, 'I leave you all my blessing, and God be with ye all for ever and ever.' He lay back on the heath and died.

" 'How long did she take to come, Father?' asked one

135

of the bystanders. 'She ran from the mouth of the Killary to Leenane in forty-eight minutes,' said the priest. This was a distance of over fourteen miles. The news of this ride spread far and wide through the barony of Ballynahinch and became part of the folklore of the region, for there is nothing in the annals of horseflesh to equal it.

"Turning to Brian, I said that if any of the Mayo rebels were present, I would appreciate his pointing them out. 'Oh, yes, I see five of them here,' he said, 'and they're seated together. Do you see that very tall, long-visaged man who is terribly pock-marked? That is Father Myles Prendergast, an Augustinian Friar from the old Abbey of Murrisk. When the French landed in Killala, Myles and another Friar named Father Michael Gannon fled from the old Abbey and joined them. Father Mick, as he was called by the peasantry, put on the uniform of a French officer, but Father Myles, who was carefree, did not put on a uniform. When the French became prisoners of war in Ballinamuck, Father Mick passed off as a French officer, and afterwards rose to be a general in Napoleon's army, while Father Myles fled to Connemara, where he lives by playing on the bagpipes at all social gatherings. [He lived to a great age and was stone-blind for many years before his death.]

" ' The strong looking, fair-haired man sitting next to Father Myles is Jimmy McGreal of Ballyhip, near Louisburgh. He led the rebels against the redcoats at the battle of Collicoon, a townland near Louisburgh. The redcoats capitulated, so the rebels took their guns and shoes, and they returned quite crestfallen to Westport. Ever since, McGreal must be called Captain McGreal. He supports himself by training gun dogs for the squireens along the sea coast.

" 'The pale-faced man with the watery eyes and long, thin nose is the loquacious, frivolous Affy Gibbons of Westport, who is a capital poet. He is the Poet Laureate of the same squireens. The young man next to him is one of the Jordans of Rosslevin, who was intended for the Church, but became a rebel. He is the tutor of the children of some squireens. [He was pardoned some years later, but was shot by Father Myles Prendergast, who suspected he was going to turn informer.] The man who sits next to him with the aquiline nose and the great blue scar on his brow, who is blind in one eye, is Jimmy Malley of Bunowen, who is always known by the nickname of 'Go-go.' He is a born soldier, and the bravest and best man I have met among the rebels.

" 'When the French laid down their arms in Ballina-muck, the British soldiers were let loose on the almost unarmed rebels who were butchered in hundreds. Those who had pikes fought bravely. As I looked around me, I saw a dragoon bearing down, sword in hand, on Go-go, who held a pike. He had nowhere to fly, so he knelt on one knee and held his long pike before him. The dragoon missed him, for he didn't wish to come too near the pike, and his horse carried him some distance before he could recover himself. Then he came thundering on once more.

" 'Go-go shortened his pike in order to tempt him, and when the dragoon drew near, the brave rebel shot out his pike and buried it in the stomach of the animal. As the horse was falling, taking his rider with him, the blow the trooper struck, although spent, struck the rebel on the forehead, gashing him from the eyebrow to the scalp.

With the spring of a panther, Go-go arose and drove his pike to the handle into the vitals of the Saxon, who fell back weltering in his gore.

" 'I hurried to Go-go's assistance and carried him to a little shrubbery nearby. I gathered some moss which I placed on the wound and tied tightly with my scarf. There he lay until night came, when I carried him towards a light I saw twinkling in the darkness. The light shone from the window of a peasant's cabin; the man bade us take shelter in his barn. There we remained for eight or nine days until the fever which raged through Go-go's body left him.

" 'Finally, he was ready to travel, and we set our faces towards the West, but, alas, it was far away below the horizon. How I led him on, how I carried him across rugged hills, through soft, interminable morasses, fens and quagmires, and deep, sluggish streams, is known only to God and myself. At the end of three weeks we arrived at the foot of Benlethry, for our goal lay two thousand feet above us in the great cave near the summit, but this climb he was unable to achieve without more assistance. I left him to seek that aid, and when I reached the cave I found some forty refugees there. Four of them went down and carried him up the mountain, and in three weeks he was quite convalescent, but he had lost an eye from the inflammation of the wound on his forehead.

" 'The man who sits next to Go-go is old Michael Sweeney, the poet, who composed 'The Wedding of Peggy O'Hara,' 'The Ghost,' and many other fine Irish songs. Beside Sweeney sits a small man dressed in a body coat of frieze, a frieze vest, and with knee-breeches over his stockings. He wears spatters, which are simply strong stockings without soles, the old Celtic legging. That man is Johnny Gibbons of Westport, the famous outlaw.' [His inordinate passion for strong drink brought him afterwards to the gallows.]

"As we looked at the famous rebels of the West, Brian sang this verse softly in my ear:

'They rose in dark and evil days
To right their native land,
They kindled here a living blaze,
That nothing shall withstand.
Alas that might
Should conquer right,
They rose and passed away,
But true men,
Like you men,
Are plenty here today.' "

THE PRINCE OF LUGATHERIV

"Let me tell you about the events of that dinner at Roger Coyne's house near Kylemore on the day of the Station," said George O'Malley, the old smuggler from Achill, as he finished a glass of punch and resumed his shanachus. "The tables were set, the viands were placed before us in abundance, and we took our places. During the repast, I kept my eyes on my plate, but once the cloth was removed I looked to see who my neighbours were, and I became greatly interested in two females who sat facing me, for their dress and manner led me to believe that they were socially far above the people around them. One of them was in the prime of life. Her fair hair lay flat and thin on her smooth, ample brow. Her face was smooth and olive-tinged, and on one of her cheeks there was a mole out of which grew a wisp of fair hair.

"Beside her sat a girl aged about twenty-two, I judged, who was the strangest girl I have ever seen. Her hair, which was on the verge of whiteness, was the colour of a bunch of primroses you would see in May in the shrubbery, or in a little dell along the banks of a river. Her face was pale, but not with the paleness of delicacy, but with that alabaster shade peculiar to blonde women. Her eyes were closed, and the long, light auburn lashes caressed her smooth cheeks. To myself I said, 'I wonder if this extraordinary girl is blind.' My curiosity was soon satisfied when the old parish priest addressed her, saying, "Nuala, my two new curates are considered the best singers among the priests of the Archdiocese; shall I get them to sing for you?' She opened her eyes and looked across at us, and as she did so, I felt myself shrivel and sink before her gaze. 'Oh! do, Father, if you please,' said she.

"Father Vaughan sang 'The Cruagh,' and Father Malley sang 'The Coolin,' not the one by Moore, but the original; old Michael Sweeney sang his own composition, 'The Wedding of Peggy O'Hara.' When Michael had finished, he said, 'When a young man I was often at the blessed well of Kilgeever, and there I was often told that Brian McNamara and his two sisters were the three best singers in Ireland. I now call on him for a song.'

"'Well, sure,' said Brian, the last Rapparee of the West, 'such as it is, you shall have it and welcome.' Brian began to sing one of the grand old love songs of Connacht, songs to which I have listened enraptured as a boy, songs which shall never be sung again by the peasantry of Ireland, for, alas, their voices are now not Irish but English. Of course, these songs have been gathered and will be sung by people in over-cultured English tones. To put it another way, to the touch it may feel like Esau, but the voice of the singer is only the voice of Jacob. Brian's grand, sonorous voice swelled out and filled the room, and was wafted by the summer night air through the narrow valley between the great mountains. There was a rush of people towards the room, where they stood in astonishment, as if listening to Ossin who had returned from Tier na Oga.

"As I looked towards the fair girl I saw that she was sitting there with her large, hazel eyes wide open, her face all radiant, and her forehead lit up as if illuminated by some bright flame inside her head, and she seemed to be in an ecstasy. When Brian ceased singing, down went the eyelids, and there she sat as still as a statue fresh and fair from the chisel of Phidias.

"The evening drew to an end, the priests took their leave, and Brian and I started on our way to my ship in the Killary. When we were some distance from the Station house, I asked him if he knew the two females. 'Oh, I have known them for years,' he replied. 'Who are they?' I asked. 'The fair one, with the mole on her left cheek, is the daughter of a Scottish nobleman who perished on the scaffold for having taken sides with the worthless pretender. She is the wife of the Prince of Lugatheriv, a glen not far off from here, and the fair young girl who sat beside her is their only child. When I get on board I will tell you all about them.'

"When we reached the ship I felt greatly fatigued as a result of not being accustomed to travelling through swamps and quagmires, for although my companion could skip over them without soiling his shoes, I would sink to the knees. Now I needed a little nourishment, and it occurred to me that a mild stimulant would be the best restorative, so I brewed a capital bowl of rum punch, which set me at peace with all mankind.

" 'Sit down, Brian, dear,' said I, 'and quaff a couple of bumpers the short while we live, and let us live and enjoy it.' 'Oh, yes, with pleasure,' said he, as he filled his tumbler and sat facing me.

"There he sat, this strange looking mortal whose enormous head of curly hair filled me with wonder, and I thought to myself that this must be how Absalom, the son of David, looked when he walked the earth. 'Now, Brian, please tell me were you serious when you said there is here in Connemara a Prince of Lugatheriv?'

" 'Why not?' asked he. 'Haven't we in Connacht a Prince of Coolavin?' 'Indeed, we have,' said I.

" 'Then why shouldn't we have a Prince of Lugatheriv?' he asked. 'Surely there is nothing extraordinary about it. The Prince of Lugatheriv is able to trace his genealogy down from the earliest pagan times to the present day, for his Pagan Firbolg ancestor, King Bola, gave the name to the great range of mountains, the Banabola, which means the gables of Bola. He fell at the great battle of Moytirra and he is buried where the Ballynahich river discharges its waters into Roundstone Bay. The townland got its name in consequence of his being buried there, and for hundreds of ages it was called Tim Bola. It is located only a mile or so from Ballynahinch

Castle. A hundred times I have passed by the great tumulus under which he lies buried.'

" 'What is the present Prince of Lugatheriv like?' I asked.

" 'He is a peasant man, but he still lives in the old feudal Castle of his ancestors which will soon be a heap of ruins, for it is greatly neglected and is hastening to decay, the more's the pity, as there was only one other like it in all Connacht. The other one belonged to Quige na Builla, mad Thady O'Flaherty, the pirate; it stood on a rock at the head of a little creek on the southern coast, some two miles from Carna, and it was called the Castle of Ard. The two castles resembled each other, for they were built in the form of a horseshoe. They looked like great Round Towers, but they were encompassed by strong walls about fourteen feet high, with a gallery or rampart all around the top.

" 'In the Prince's Castle, which stands on a rock on the western bank of Lough Inagh above which towers the stupendous Ben Bawn, there are pricelsss treasures in the shape of old curios, some of them at least 3,000 years old, which he would not exchange for the richest Crown in Europe. In a room in his Castle he could show you the Cotha More which his ancestor, King Bola, wore at the battle of Moytirra. He could show you the Caubeen stuffed with hay which the grand old monarch wore on that fatal day. These great heirlooms the Prince always wears when on the war-path.

" 'He could show you the great war club of wild mountain holly with which Bola severed the arm from the shoulder of the Danann King, Nuagha, who ever afterwards wore a silver arm and was named therefore

Airgiod Lamh. In a grand old wooden Mather of superior workmanship, the Prince has stored some of the brain balls which his glorious ancestors cast with much precision and fatal effect at their enemies. It was with one of these oval-shaped balls that one of my ancestors struck Conor MacNessa and disabled him for life, the false-hearted villain, and this missile at last caused his death, which was well-deserved, in consequence of his treachery towards the children of Usnach.

" 'One of the most interesting souvenirs of Pagan times is a wooden vessel which the Prince calls a goloon, which is filled with three-cornered little pieces like pieces of English slates. It was with these diabolical, magical missiles that the Tuatha De Dananns annihilated the Firbolgs, my ancestors, for the De Dananns were magicians, and by their art they were capable of raising showers of hailstones which always came with the north wind. Among the hailstones these three-cornered pieces came and fell, and woe to the man or beast that got even a touch of one.

" 'The blow or touch was almost imperceptible, but small as it was, the man or beast was a corpse before the sun went down. These vile things were called sythes by the ancients and were the terror of the peasantry of Ireland even in Christian times. This was a nice mild way of denuding Ireland of its people, and is practised by the English of our time in another mild form, eviction, emigration and the poor house. Of course, my ancestors often rose against the Dananns, but it was of no avail, for when our people were wounded by them, they remained so, whereas when my ancestors wounded the Dananns, they gathered a hundred white cows; then they dug a pond, milked the cows into it and bathed in the milk.

Then they arose from the milk bath, quite healed of their wounds!'

"This piece of shanachus aroused my curiosity to a terrible pitch, so I said to him, 'Brian, you must take me to see the Prince and his Castle tomorrow.'

" 'Very good,' said he, 'I shall do so with pleasure.'

" 'Now,' said I, 'tell me all about his wife who, you say, is the daughter of a Scotch nobleman who died for the Stuarts.'

" "The last effort the Scotch made, I think, was headed by the Earl of March assisted by Lord Lovat,' Brian said. 'Of course, this effort failed, and Lord Lovat was arrested and perished on the scaffold. His wife, who was far gone in pregnancy, fled from Scotland on board a Connemara smuggling vessel. The smuggler landed her in his native Ballyconree on the West coast, some three miles from where there now stands the town of Clifden. She told her story to the villagers who, with the hospitality for which they are proverbial, built her a rude cabin and furnished it with food and fuel. When the time came for her to be delivered and labour set in, there she was without means or money, without a fond mother to rush to her assistance in this most critical crisis of her life. She knelt in the rude cabin with great drops of perspiration brought on by the pangs of travail standing out on her noble brow and trickling down her emaciated, tear-stained, once beautiful cheeks. When the time came, she gave birth to twins, a male and a female, and then she swooned away as if she were dead.

" 'There she lay on her rude stone pallet with her fatherless twins beside her. Can you realize the condition of this exile who was so luxuriously reared, the daughter of an Earl, the beloved and cherished wife of a Lord, whose gory head she saw raised aloft in the hands of the executioner as he cried out, 'Behold the head of a rebel!'

" 'Many months went by after childbirth before she became convalescent, and then she determined to endeavour to support herself and her orphans by the labour of her hands. She became what the peasantry called a mantimaker. As time went on, her little ones began to toddle about, and soon she saw with dismay that her son, Simon Fraser, the heir of many titles, was blind. His hair was white; the peasantry of those days called such children Dall Bawns. The little girl was without blemish. The noble lady decided to counteract the evil to her son, so she began to teach the blind boy how to support himself against the day when she would be laid to rest for ever in some lonely graveyard in this strange land far away from the land of her childhood and youth. She took out the war-pipes of her dear, dead husband, and began to teach the blind boy how to play them, for she was a skilled musician.

" 'Often through the long days, the noble lady would cease plying her needle in the art of the mantimaker, letting her beautifully shaped hands fall into her lap. Then would she cast her eyes towards her beloved Caledonia and sigh and weep, and the great, blue mountains of Scotland, the broad lakes, the rapid rivers, would appear before her. Then too would she see the form and face of her dead husband, and her beloved parents, and her brothers and sisters, and then the tears would fall once more.

" 'Since she was a courageous as well as an educated lady, she taught her little girl to read and write English and French. Meanwhile she was much annoyed by the attentions of would-be suitors whom she repelled with scorn. How similar was her case to that of Sarah Curran!

She is far from the land where her young hero sleeps
And lovers around her are sighing;
But coldly she turns from their gaze and weeps,
For her heart in his cold grave is lying.
He had lived for his love, for his country he died,
They were all that to life had entwined him,
Nor soon shall the tears of his country be dried,
Nor long shall his love stay behind him.

" 'As her children began to grow up, Lady Lovat began to decline, and when they were fully able to support themselves, she took to her bed and soon died.

O, make her grave where the moonbeams rest,
Where they promise a glorious morrow,
They will shine o'er her grave like a ray from
the West,
From her own dear island of sorrow.

" 'At that time, all tailors went from house to house making the clothes of the peasantry, and the mantimakers worked in a similar manner. When her mother died, her daughter, Miss Fraser, began to go from village to village as a dress or mantimaker. She wandered on towards the distant, towering Bunabola mountains, and was employed by the inhabitants who lived in the little hamlet of Lugatheriv. Here the young Prince met her, fell in love, and married her. He was a very rich man then. When the sister had left her mother's cabin, the blind boy began to go around through all the villages of his native barony, then and long afterwards. He was passionately fond of music, and he earned his living as a piper.'

" 'Now, Brian, please tell me all that you know about that fair girl, the Prince's daughter, who sat beside her lovely mother tonight at the Station dinner.'

" 'Not tonight,' he replied with a sigh. 'This much will I tell you, that I saved her life. I kept her from a horrid death, but her parents are unaware of this. On some other occasion I shall relate this tale to you.' "

THE RESCUE OF NULA O'FLAHERTY

"When the Rapparee, Brian McNamara, informed me that he had saved the life of the daughter of the Prince of Lugatheriv," said old George O'Malley, the smuggler from Achill, "I became very much interested and longed to learn how he did it. In daytime aboard the lugger, Brian observed the greatest reticence, but when night set in and he had partaken of the fourth tumbler of punch, he was the best after-dinner talker I had ever met. In fact, he would be brimming over with anecdotes and legendary lore, and he could be coaxed on to sharing it by the invigorating juice of the barley which makes the best punch in creation. In fact," said the old smuggler, while his aged face lit up with a broad smile, "if you get the genuine Iska Baha, there isn't a headache in ten gallons of it. After dinner one night on the ship moored in the Killary, I mixed a capital bowl of the genuine punch, for by this time I knew it was Brian's favourite beverage, and I found that it would make him loquacious.

" 'That's capital stuff,' he said, after he had tasted a glass. 'Is it strong enough?' I asked. 'If not, I shall throw in another weesha cropper.' 'Oh, no, it's grand,' he replied. 'Well, then, help yourself, avick; don't spare it, for, thank God, there is more corn in Egypt,' I said.

"Then I began to draw him out. 'It's a wonder to me,' I said, 'that the fair young girl has not met some of the young Squireens along the seacoast trying to put their come-hither on her.'

" 'There is not a young fellow of note in the parish of Ballinakill or the parish of Ballinadoon and Omey but is after her,' he said. 'The Coneys, the Bodkins, the Darcys, the Corbets, the Slopers, and the poets and poetasters have all vied with each other in singing her praises. Affy Gibbons, the rebel poet, composed a song in her praise, but the peasantry only laughed at him, for he is too ponderous, affecting the style of Pope and Addison. It was not so with the song which Michael Sweeney composed in her honour, for it is sung both in Galway and Mayo even to this day. Sweeney, you know, was the Robert Burns of Connacht, and always composed in Irish and English, for he was a fair scholar, although he only learned in what is called a hedge school, which I hold are the best schools in the world.

" 'The peasantry of Sweeney's day who could read and write were far and away the best and cleverest men Ireland has produced since, or ever will produce again, and I shall prove it. It is true that they never learned English grammar, but I hold that too much polishing wears away a thing, rendering it almost worthless, and I hold that too much polishing also wears away the human mind and deprives it of much of its natural vigour. The hedge schoolboys hadn't a regular set of school books, so they took with them to school every sort of book they could lay hands on.

" 'The hedge schoolmaster was not the sort of man whom Carleton and Lever have lampooned, no such thing; he was generally a well-informed stranger, the scion perhaps of some noble family who had been disinherited by Elizabeth, or by James the First, or by the inhuman Cromwell. The school boys carried with them to these masters Homer's *Iliad* and *Odyssey*, *Paradise Lost* and *Paradise Regained*, the *History of Greece and Rome*, the *Arabian Nights*, Thomas-a-Kempis, Dr. Gallagher and Keating, the *Old Testament*, Salust in English, Ovid, Ward's *Cantos*, McGeoghegan's *History of Ireland*, and a hundred and one other books. Where they all came from is one of the things that now astonishes me, for these books were in every peasant's cottage on the little loft over the fireplace, along with the wool-cards, the balls of yarn, and the spindles; there the books rested, some without covers, and all of them stained with smoke. When a boy had his *Odyssey* read, he exchanged it with another chap for his *Iliad*, and so on. They spent seven or eight years at this kind of work, and got them off by heart, as we called it.

" 'Each boy and girl had a favourite Grecian or Roman hero; some admired Socrates, some Leonidas, some Lycurgus, some Xenophon, and some Cincinnatus. The girls were taught to admire Susanna, Judith, the mother of the Machabees, Lucretia, and Virginia, while we all admired Hannibal. Often we had refined boxing matches, with each boy standing up for his favourite hero. This business was conducted according to the rules of the ring, for we had two seconds and a timekeeper, whose business it was to see that one boy didn't hit the other below the belt, or when he was down.

" 'The children were also taught how to sit at table, and how to handle a knife and fork. They were taught to salute and respect the aged, and to bow and draw their bob or forelock to all strangers; anyhow, the bob got its own share of pulling, for, alas, we had no cap to raise. When these ragged little boys, some wearing trousers, some wearing flannel petticoats, or dresses like females, left off going to school and began to handle their spades, their minds were made. In fact, they had the minds of fully-grown, noble men and women, for, to their credit, let it be said that some of the girls were the cleverest in the schools.

" 'These little boys and girls when they left school were better informed than the fully grown men of the present day. One of them knew more about the world than all the National School boys in the parish if they were all melted down and cast into one huge National School boy of this day. It was in these hedge schools that the Irish peasantry learned to be steadfast, honourable and truthful, and to have fortitude, so that when the penal laws and the persecution set in, they thought of the woman and her seven sons in the Bible, of Daniel in the lion's den, and the fiery furnace, and they held to the faith of their fathers like grim death, and won. I wonder, if the penal laws and the persecution set in now in this frivolous age with its threepenny novels, novelettes, and penny horror tales, would we be able to give such a good account of ourselves. Indeed, I fear not.

" 'It was in these hedge schools that the Four Masters first learned to read and write. It was in these schools that Dr. O'Higgins of Ardagh learned to be a grand Bishop and a great patriot, and last, but not least, it was in a hedge school that the Lion of the fold of Juda, the illustrious John McHale of Tuam, first learned to be a great prelate, a noble patriot, and a melodious poet. And it was in one of these schools that old Michael Sweeney, the peasant-poet, learned to compose in two languages, and in later life to sing so simply and yet so sweetly the charms of Nula O'Flaherty, the fair daughter of the Prince of Lugatheriv.'

"Brian sang the words then in his glorious voice:
'In Ballynahinch there lies
A maid of great surprise,
No beauty can exceed this damsel's,
The beams that from her eyes
Would dazzle all your sight,
Like Phoebus of a summer's morning;
She's fairer than the swan,
She's milder than the lamb,
She's beautiful, discreet and charming,
And if she went to Rotterdam,
I'd follow her by land,
Sweet Murneen, Nagroga Bawna.'

"'All of Sweeney's songs can be found in Hardiman's *Bardic Remains of Ireland*,' said the Rapparee as he drained his sixth tumbler, and yet he was quite sober and in grand talking trim.

"'Now, Brian, dear,' said I, 'talking is dry work; help yourself again, avick, and tell me how you saved the life of this lovely girl.'

"He filled his seventh tumbler and then began: 'When we fled from Ballinamuck, we all made for the great cave of Benlethry, and there we almost starved. Besides, we knew that Dick Martin had a regiment of yeomen in

152

Ballynahinch Castle, which lay beyond the lake at the foot of the mountain, so, you see, we were in a sad plight. When I lived in Mayo, I used to do a fair share of shooting, and I learned to shoot straight, for why should a man fire unless he is sure to kill the object he fires at, when the report of firearms could bring two or three spies and gamekeepers around? Never fire if you don't know how to kill.

" 'Luckily, I had a gun, and I knew that the mountains abounded with wild goats; they were domestic ones at one time, and belonged to a hag who lived in one of the glens at the foot of Benbawn. The old hag was called Colagh na Gowar by the peasants; she had no family, so when she died the goats ran wild, for there were no relatives to claim them. Benbawn has many cliffs on whose terraces the goats were to be seen in hundreds, huge animals with long hair which swept the ground. When we were almost famished from hunger, I took out my gun, which was a snipe gun with a very small bore, true and accurate as a rifle.

" 'I had a long distance to travel around by Eaur na Noran and along the brow of the great, dark mountain Glankohin, and then I began to climb towards the cliff which overhangs the wild woods of Derryclare and the ever beautiful Lough Inagh. I cut the balls I used into four pieces, as you would an orange, and then I tied these pieces together with a thin, cotton thread before loading the barrel, so that when the charge struck the object fired at, the thread would burst, with the result that there would be four wounds instead of one. On my first day, I killed four goats. Some of the starving outlaws followed me and took the corpses of the goats to the cave; from

153

that day forward we had plenty of goat flesh.

" 'One day as I was traversing a deep glen from which arose a steep precipice, I heard the heart-rending cry of a woman, and as I looked above me I saw a girl rushing headlong down the craggy mountainside towards the cliff. She was being pursued by an enormous buck goat. When she reached the brow of the cliff, she sent up another wail. The infuriated animal rose on his hind legs to strike her, but in doing so, he exposed his vital parts towards me, and I shot him through the heart so that he fell with a great thud at my feet. He was the largest animal of his species on earth, for when the men came and broke him up, they found twelve stone of tallow in him.

" 'When the girl realized her position, she became unnerved and sat down on the brow of the beetling cliff and sent up another cry. Fearing that she would plunge headlong into the glen below, I put down my gun and began to climb towards her. It was a perilous undertaking, but it had to be done, and I had learned climbing in my youth on the most precipitous mountain in Ireland, my own native, darling Mweelrea. When I reached the girl, I put my left arm around her waist and led her down the steep, slippery declivity with great care.

" 'At last we reached the glen where the girl sat down on a boulder and looked up at me with her large, hazel eyes. As I gazed at her, I thought that she was surely the strangest girl I had ever seen, so tall and young, and with unusual hair. 'Sir,' she said, 'you have saved my life twice over, and you are a wonderful brave man. I am greatly upset, so I am unable to express my gratitude sufficiently, but when I recover, I shall do so. Please tell me who you are.'

"'I am one of the outlaws, one of the refugees dwelling in the cave of Benlethry,' I replied. 'Very well, I shall call to see you and thank you there,' she said, 'on the last Sunday in summer.' 'Why on that particular day?' I asked. 'Do you see that great mountain beyond the lake?' she asked. 'Yes, I do,' said I. 'On the South of that mountain, which overhangs Recess, there is a holy well some two thousand feet above sea level; it is called Tubber Patrick, St. Patrick's Well,' she answered. 'On the last Sunday in summer there is a pattern held there which is surely the greatest in Ireland, and my parents will be there on that day, so I will have an opportunity of calling to the cave.' 'Please tell me your name,' I asked. 'I am the daughter of the Prince of Lugatheriv,' she said, as she arose and went down the mountain towards the old Castle.'

"Then," said the old smuggler, "I asked the Rapparee if he had ever been at that pattern." 'Oh yes,' he replied, 'I have been there often. Where it is held is called Maun Ean, or the gap or gorge of the birds, because the mountains are so high that the birds when migrating North or South must fly through this gap in the range of mountains. The pattern is held on Garland Sunday, which the peasants call Doomagh Crom Duff. It is the greatest gathering of people I ever saw, and the most heterogeneous. They come from far-off Partry, from the banks of the Corrib, from the Joyce Country and Maam, from Oughterard, Carraro, Rosmuck, Carna, Roundstone, Errisbeg, Errismore, and Ballinakill, the wildest people in creation.

"They come on Saturday and spend the night in the open air dancing, singing, and drinking poteen. Next morning they give their station, as they term it, and then

155

they amuse themselves by engaging in the most terrific faction fights I have ever seen. It is often that men go to this Pattern of Maum Ean in perfect health and vigour, without a blemish, in order to distinguish themselves; they spend the night as I have described, and on the next day return home maimed and disfigured for life, some having their skulls bashed in, some having lost an eye, and some having a broken nose or a broken arm or leg. They could be seen about four o'clock on that afternoon, many with their heads bound up in turban fashion with the small, woollen neck shawls of their wailing mothers, wives, or sisters, who were leading them tenderly and carefully down along the steep mountain side, all the while scolding and upbraiding them as they descended.

" 'Now, Columb,' they would say, 'we often told you to keep away from the Pattern of Maum Ean, but you would not hear us. What will you do now that you have an eye lost?' 'Oh,' the man would reply, 'what about the loss of an eye when I have my soul saved, for didn't I give my station at the blessed well at sunrise, with the help of God and St. Patrick?' He would stumble for a moment in weakness and then continue, 'I wish every poor sinner in Ireland were in the state of grace and perfection I am in at this moment, but, forear gare they aren't.' Another woman would be saying to her darling son, 'Now, Greeora, what will you do when your nose is gone, for Nappy Tolan won't marry you, but she will surely marry your rival, Dudley Cloherty.' 'I will marry no girl in Ireland until I have blood for blood, and I shall have it at the next fair of Ballynahinch, or in Roundstone on Saints Peter and Paul's Day,' he would bellow.

"Have you seen any of these fights?" I asked Brian.

'Oh, yes,' he answered. 'I have seen the great fights between the Joyces of Joyce Country and the Malleys of
Maam, and on the same day the battle between the Kings
of Errisbeg and the Mannions of Cashel. These were the
two greatest fights of modern times. The Joyces challenged the Malleys to fight them in Maumean or Doomagh Crom Duff. The news spread far and wide, so there
was a vast multitude of both sexes gathered on that day.

" 'The Joyces were the largest men I have ever seen,
that is, each of them had a body as large as a feather-bed,
and when I looked at them, for I have a critical eye for
matters of this sort, I knew they would be beaten, for
they were too unwieldy; they lacked suppleness and
vigour, the two most essential qualifications of fighting
men. The O'Malleys were about the smallest men to be
seen anywhere, but they had the dash and vigorous
energy of men who are determined to conquer, and they
succeeded, for the Joyces were about the worst men I
have ever seen in a faction fight.

" 'The Joyces drew up in the order of battle, but made
no effort to assail their foes, so the intrepid O'Malleys
began the attack, led on by a very small, neat, fair-haired
man, who turned out to be the most expert man with a
stick I ever saw. The Joyces went down before them like
stooks of corn in a storm, and in ten or fifteen minutes
there wasn't a man named Joyce but lay stretched out on
the heather, while the O'Malleys stood over them, thrashing them as though they were dusting carpets.

" 'Then the other fight began between the Kings of
Errisbeg and the Mannions of Cashel. The Kings were
great, stout men, but the Mannions were the tallest men,
I dare say, in Connacht. This was surely the battle of the

gods and giants, and they fought on until the shades of night separated them, nor was the fight decided on that day, for it was to be renewed at the next fair at Ballynahinch.'

"Bedad, Brian," said I, "the Pattern of Maum Ean is a very dangerous spot."

" 'It is seldom any man went there who ever returned without a wound,' he replied.

"And what did you do, Brian, dear," I asked, "when you saw that darling girl again on the Pattern Day, or did you ever see her at all?"

" 'Musha,' said Brian, stretching and yawning, 'it's tired out I am entirely. That will keep to another day.' "

THE TRIBUTE OF KING O'TOOLE

"On a calm evening when the western sun was sinking behind the great blue mountains," said George O'Malley, the old smuggler, "I brewed a bowl of strong barley punch that Brian liked so well, and after he had taken a few glasses, I said to the last Rapparee of the West, 'I wonder does the wife of the Prince of Lugatheriv ever visit her mother's grave in Omey Island?'

" 'I don't know that,' he said, 'but I know that I went there, not to see the woman's grave, but to see the graveyard which was the scene of a very historic battle.' 'Please tell me about it,' I said.

" 'Oh, I'll tell you with pleasure,' said he. 'Some two hundred years ago, Omey Island was ruled by a monarch named King O'Toole, a grand potentate, not the old fellow who owned the celebrated gander, but far and

away a greater monarch. At this time the Chief King of
Iar Connacht lived in the great feudal Castle of Aughna
Noor, which stood on the bank of the Corrib, and whose
walls are quite perfect evern to this day, the greatest and
grandest ruin I have ever seen. This chieftain was named
Morragh n-Thua, or of the hatchet, who held sway from
the Corrib to the Atlantic. One day he sent envoys to
King O'Toole demanding tribute.

" "When the envoys reached the palace of King O'Toole,
the grand old king was preparing to have lunch; he was
a single old gentleman who had never married, and consequently he did all the culinary work himself like all old
bachelors. He was just baking forty large potatoes in the
hot ashes and cinders; when they were thoroughly done,
he took them out and carefully wiped them, then he
scraped the crust with the Sheen Duff which hung from
his girdle. He then took a deep wooden bowl or dish and
put all the potatoes into it, save the skin, which, when I
was a wee chap, we called the pluckie, and which our
ancestors looked upon as a delicacy, and always served for
dessert. When the King was ready, he took about half a
pound of old crock butter, and melted and mingled it
with the potatoes, mashing them up together. This
savoury dish was called bruteen. Doctors aver that this
sort of pudding causes wind on the stomach, so King
O'Toole must have often ruffled the waters around Omey
Island.

" 'The King next opened the family chest and took out
a noggin of goat's milk. He sat down in his straw sheet-
ogue or arm-chair, placed the noggin on one knee, the
dish on the other, and helped himself to a wee lunch. He
never could tolerate having a table in the palace. While

he was engaged in eating, two tall pigs stood facing him in the centre of the chamber, vociferously squealing, demanding a portion of the savoury dish. In the door there stood two large goats with their hind feet on the threshhold, and their fore ones resting on the closed half-door; their large horns touched the lintel, and their venerable beards fell down over their breasts. There they stood, for all the world like two old withered Oriental astrologers contemplating the stars.

" 'When the old monarch had finished his light repast, he arose with dignity, shook out and adjusted his regal robes, and addressed the envoys who had been waiting all this time. 'Whence come ye?' he asked them. 'We have come from the great Castle of Aughna Noor,' said they. 'Why?' asked he. 'We came to demand tribute from you for our master, the great King Murragh O'Flaherty.' 'Return to your master,' said the monarch, 'and tell him to come for it himself, and if he comes to Omey, I shall give him the soundest thrashing he ever got in his life, the plunderin' villain.'

" 'Then King O'Toole began to prepare for war, for well he knew Murragh would invade his dominion. He possessed no arms or weapons of any kind, so he gathered about a hundred cart loads of paving stones which he caused to be piled in lumps above high water mark along the strand. Then he visited his arsenal, which contained one old firelock. It was once a flint one, but the lock and hammer were gone, and the barrel had fallen from the stock.

" 'The King consulted his chief sharpshooter, Festy Folan. 'Look at that, Festy,' he said. 'Well, I see it,' answered Festy. 'Do you think it will do?' asked the

160

King. 'It will when I twine it,' said Festy. 'But where is the twine to come from when I have none?' asked the King, shaking his head. 'Oh, I'll get some twine,' answered the sharpshooter.

" 'In the sand hills of Omey there grew a tall kind of wild grass which sends roots through the sand a hundred feet long. These roots are as fine and tough as twine, so Festy bound the old gun together with this rude substitute for twine. Then he called his assistant, Darby Cloherty. 'Go down to the rock which is above high-water mark on the strand and build a small fire beside it,' he said. You can see that King O'Toole was determined not to be caught napping by the invader; in fact, he was thoroughly equipped for war.

" 'When the envoys reached Aughna Noor, Murragh asked them if they had seen King O'Toole. 'We did,' they answered. 'Arra, musha, what sort is he?' the King demanded. 'Oh, he lives in great state,' said they. 'When we reached the palace, he was taking his lunch, and the table he used he would not sell or part with for all the gold you ever handled. While he was eating, there were two musicians standing facing him, playing the war pipes, and the music they made could be heard two miles away. In the door there stood two halbert men on guard, their bright spears touching the lintel, while their long beards covered their breasts.'

" 'By gob,' said Murragh, 'he must be a great fellow. What did he say when ye demanded tribute?' 'He said if he were near you he'd give you a sound thrashing,' replied the envoys. So O'Flaherty began to rage. 'I will drag himself and his subjects in chains and cast them into Cishlan na irka, in the lake shall I cast them, and let them

161

starve,' said the King. He gathered his troops about him in order to start for the far West the next morning.

" 'At this time Murragh had two grown daughters, one of whom was engaged to be married to the Earl of Clanrichard who was just then on a visit to Aughna Noor. Next morning Murragh set out for Omey Island accompanied by his two daughters, his prospective son-in-law, Clanrichard, and a vast army. In the afternoon they reached Claddagh Duff. When they looked towards Omey, they could see King O'Toole and his army drawn up along the shore. 'The savages haven't even a black thorn in their hands,' said Clanrichard. 'We shall have an easy vistory,' said Murragh.

" 'At full tide, a bay almost a mile wide separates Omey Island from Claddagh Duff on the mainland. At low water the channel is a vast strand stretching off towards the South. When the spring tides begin to flow, the flood water rushes in with terrific force and rapidity, but the inland invaders knew nothing about matters of this sort. The strand was almost covered with the flood tide when the invaders began to cross over.

" 'All this time Festy Folan knelt beside the rock on the beach, his old gun laid on the rock; beside the rock his assistant had a fire in which he had the half of an old tongs, the end of which was a fierce red colour. 'Have you the iron rod?' said the gunner. 'I have,' answered the other. 'Now I am going to take aim,' said Festy, 'so when I put my left hand behind me, you will put the red iron on the pan in which there is some powder; do you understand?' 'I do,' he replied.

" 'Festy took deliberate aim; he put his left hand behind him. There came the loud report of a firearm, and Murragh O'Flaherty of Aughna Noor fell out of the saddle, shot dead through the heart. With the rapidity of lightning, Festy charged again. 'Have you the iron in the fire?' he said. There was another loud report, and the Earl of Clanrichard of Punthuma Castle fell out of the saddle, shot dead also through the heart.

" 'The horsemen turned and fled, with the water reaching up to their saddle girths. The infantry was then quite near the beach where they were cornered and assailed by King O'Toole and his army, who pelted them unmercifully with paving stones, killing them by the score. Then they looked behind them, but a broad bay lay between them and Claddagh Duff. There they stood between the devil and the deep sea, and they perished to a man.

" 'Next morning there were six hundred corpses at high water mark on the strand of Omey Island. They were never buried until the wild sea birds tore them to pieces, and they rotted there. The stench was so great that the spot and the graveyard beside it were called "Ola Breana" or stinking oil, a name it retains to this day. Thus fell ignobly Murragh the Great of Aughna Noor and his prospective son-in-law, Clanrichard, in a mean squabble, which was surely the greatest disaster recorded in traditional Irish history.'

"Brian, Brian, musha," I said, "where on earth did you get all this shanachus?"

" 'Tis a gift from the gods,' said he. Then he tossed off a last tumbler of punch, took off his garments, retired to his bunk, and was soon fast asleep."

"One evening when we were comfortably seated in the cabin of the lugger," said the old smuggler, George O'Malley, "we placed our steaming glasses before us, and then I asked Brian McNamara what he meant when he told me once that the Prince of Lugatheriv, when on the war-path, wore the Cothamore of his ancestors. 'Surely, I said, 'there is no war now going on in Connemara.'

" 'Not now," he replied, 'but at election time there is always a war, and a terrible one it is too, between the Martins of Ballynahinch and the Frenches of Porta-carran.'

" 'Are the Frenches able to stand up against Dick Martin?' I asked.

" 'Caesar French is a top match for Dick Martin, or for George Robert Fitzgerald of Turlough, for he fought both of them. He is considered the best shot in Ireland,' Brian said, 'and none dare stand before him with a sword. Of course, neither of these men is worth a curse at close quarters in a faction fight, or trial of strength. The Prince of Lugatheriv would brain a hundred such men, for he stands six feet, ten inches in his stockings. In fact, were it not for the Prince, Dick Martin would never be able to stand up against the Frenches, for what Ney was to Napoleon, this man is to Martin, his right hand and the bravest of the brave. The peasantry of the hills look upon him as their hereditary chief, and four hundred mount-aineers follow him to battle.'

" 'Have you seen any of these battles?' I asked.

" 'Yes, I have seen the last one that was held, and surely that was the Waterloo of the Frenches,' he replied.

'When the last election was going to take place, both sides began to prepare months before the election day arrived, for this was to be the final struggle to see who would be supreme despot of West Galway. Both the Martins and the Frenches had estates in that terrible, wild region, and it was there that the best fighting men were to be had, those fair-haired men of enormous stature. Two-thirds of them at least belonged to Martin, whilst most of French's followers came from the country around the Corrib.

" 'French also had the sympathy of the inhabitants of the old city, for he claimed and prided himself as being one of the Tribes; consequently, the Claddagh fishermen, of whom there were nearly two thousand, always fought beneath his banner. In the Claddagh in those days there were six hundred boats, and each boat had a crew of three, so it was not a light job to face them. But it was their wives who did the most harm to Martin's followers. They came in hundreds, carrying skibs of filth and offal poised gracefully on their heads, and in the heat of action they cast their vile missiles in the eyes of Martin's followers, blinding them.

" 'When Martin was prepared to start for Galway on the day of the election, he was placed in a position which caused him much mental disturbance, for his wife clung to him and would not let him go. She had a presentiment, she said, that he would never return to her alive. Of course, he had to go, so he set out, after embracing her; when he had gone, she swooned away and was carried to her chamber by her maids. Because Martin was too impulsive and too sanguine, he set out without waiting for the Prince of Lugatheriv to join him, and soon he, like all hasty men, found his mistake. The Prince was quite a different kind of man; he knew this would be a final effort, so he didn't leave until he made certain he would win, determined as he was to leave nothing to chance.

" 'When all was ready, the Prince rushed down the mountain towards the doomed city like Brennus and his Gauls bursting down the Alps to reduce Rome to ashes. Behind him ran four hundred fighting men, and behind them came a hundred Amazons, led by big Anna Connelly of Derryconly, the most ferocious and terrible woman who has ever figured in West Connacht. Each of these fierce women carried a new Connemara stocking, in the sole of which there slumbered a paving stone of some two pounds weight, a blow from which was almost as fatal as a pebble cast from the sling of a David.

" 'When Dick Martin reached Galway, his men were greatly fatigued after their march of forty miles, while French's men were fresh. French attacked Martin's forces as they entered the town and drove them back towards Moycullen where they formed a cordon across the road to hold them back. But this state did not last too long, for the Prince was seen coming to their assistance. Martin's men sent up a great shout and opened a passage for the Prince. On he came dressed out in his full fighting rig, Cothamore and Caubeen, and in his hand he carried his great club of wild mountain holly.

" 'French's courage failed him, and he ran for dear life towards the city, followed by his panic-stricken followers. He ran until he reached a little square in the centre of the city, where he rallied his disheartened troops. This square is formed by the meeting of four streets, namely

Upper and Lower Cross Streets, High Street and Quay, the latter of which runs down to the broad, rapid river, across which there is an old wooden bridge which connects the town with the Claddagh, and it was across this bridge and along this street that the fish wives always came to French's assistance, with their baskets of filth. The battle raged in the square for some time, with French casting many an anxious look towards the Claddagh, expecting the women to pour across the bridge. They did not fail him on this occasion, but when they entered Quay Street they saw a sight that they never forgot to their dying day.

" 'They saw big Anna Connelly and her hundred demons come rushing at them, mowing them down by the scores, so that in a few moments Quay Street was strewn with wounded women, all besmeared and covered with the filth they intended for others. All who escaped from this treatment fled across the old bridge, nor did they look behind them until they reached their little homes in the Claddagh, where they bolted themselves securely. Then big Anna swung around through the fish market and entered Flood Street through the Spanish Parade. When French's followers saw those enraged Amazons approaching, a panic set in; they fled towards the green, and some ran to Claregalway, while others rushed towards Cranmore.

" 'French retired to Portacarran, which became his St. Helena, and Flood Street, which was then the principal thoroughfare of Galway, was wrecked and in ruins. That evening Dick Martin was M.P. and Director of West Galway, and the Prince of Lugatheriv, his four hundred

warriors and his hundred Amazons returned in triumph
to the dark blue mountains.' "

THE UNWRITTEN LAW

"I could see that Brian had a story he wanted to tell
me," said George O'Malley, the smuggler from Achill,
"so I filled his glass once more, and encouraged him to
loosen his golden tongue. 'Brian, dear,' said I, 'you're a
grand man with the shanachus, and you must have many
stories of Connemara to tell me.'

" 'Well,' said he, 'as my name is Brian McNamara,
and I come from a long and noble line, I have kept stored
in my mind the legends of the people. There is a tale about
a proud, wronged man that I will give you now. On the
night when Dick Martin returned in triumph to Ballynahinch after his election as M.P. for Galway, he visualized
the welcome he would receive from his dear wife, how
she would throw her arms around his neck, kiss him and
press him to her loving, fond heart, a heart which had
almost burst with sorrow at his departure for Galway for
the election battle. These reflections caused him to hasten
on his journey, so that when he reached the Castle he had
cause to cry out like the Prince of Brefiny:

'The valley lay smiling before me,
 When lately I left her behind,
 Yet I trembled and something hung o'er me
 That saddened the joy of my mind.
 I looked for the lamp that she told me
 Would shine when her hero returned,
 Though darkness began to enfold me,
 No lamp from the battlement burned.

I flew to the chamber, 'twas lonely,
  As if the loved tenant lay dead;
Ah! would it were death, or death only!
  But no, the young false one had fled,
And there hung the lute that might soften
  My very worst pains into bliss,
While the hand that had waked it so often
  Now throbbed to a proud rival's kiss.'

" 'When Dick Martin reached the Castle, he found that his faithless wife had eloped with another man, and who that man was he did not know. All that he could learn was that a ship sailed up Roundstone Bay and cast anchor within a mile of the Castle in the little bay of Cloonisle, that Mrs. Martin was seen leaving the Castle at midnight, that she was seen going on board the ship, and that soon the ship set sail, and not another trace was there of the lady of the Castle.

" 'Dick Martin decided to travel through Europe in search of the fleeing pair, disguised as an Oriental diamond merchant; he took with him a faithful native servant named Jimmy Pearl, who carried the pack of goods. Martin adopted a strict rule from which he never deviated; he would never display the rare trinkets save to the lady of the mansion which he visited. He set out on his travels, first searching every city of note and every great manor house in Ireland, without avail. Next he searched all England, Scotland and Wales, but not a clue could be found in any of these places.

" 'Finally, he crossed over to France, determined to search Paris first. On the night he arrived there was a great ball at the palace of some nobleman to which all the nobility of Paris were invited, so Mr. Martin went there to watch the arrivals. This ball far excelled the great ball given years afterwards in Brussels, and ended far more tragically.

> 'There was a sound of revelry by night
> And France's capital had gathered there
> Her beauty and her chivalry, and bright
> The lamps shone o'er fair women and brave men,
> A thousand hearts beat happily, and when
> Music arose with its voluptuous swell,'

Dick Martin rushed in among the throng of whirling dancers, pistol in hand, closely followed by his faithful servant, who carried a loaded pistol, also. There was a sharp crack, and the hostess, who was Martin's faithless wife, fell back, shot through the heart. The betrayed husband took the other pistol from his man and shot her seducer through the brain, and he also fell back, dead.

" 'Of course, a panic set in, and all the guests stampeded towards the door. The old Dowagers, the Duchesses and the Countesses first ran, but it was their corpulency which brought about the terrible catastrophe which followed, for two of the Dowagers met in the doorway and got wedged together in such a manner as to prevent the guests from getting out of the room, nor could any human effort force them asunder. The melee began in earnest, for the old Dowagers tore each other to pieces. They tore off each other's false hair; they tore out each other's false eyes and teeth, tore off their coronets and crowns, while the paint on their wrinkled faces began to melt with the perspiration, making them hideous to look at.

" 'Then the fair, almost naked debutantes made a rush for the door. Unable to force their way out, they became desperate and tore their scanty drapery to pieces. There they stood, as nude as Eve in the Garden of Eden, nor did they seem to be disconcerted by their appearance. During all this time, the gentlemen were not idle, for in seeking an outlet from the room, they tore off their willie-wagtail coats, their low-cut vests, the great white shirt-fronts; then the neat white trousers without any hose inside fell to the ground, and to complete the devastation, the well-kept imperials and well-waxed moustaches were plucked out and flung on the floor. There they stood, naked and shivering, knee-deep in the most valuable heap of clothing and gems which they trampled on as worthless possessions compared with one hour's freedom in the open air. There they stood, shivering and appalled before one brave man who had administered the unwritten law to two villains who had disgraced and dishonoured him, for whom he had searched for four long, weary years.

" 'When the two Dowagers were at long last extricated from the door, they were stark dead and disfigured beyond recognition, for they scraped and tore at each other to the bitter end. They were gone to their eternal reward amid the evergreen bowers of the Elysian fields where, let us hope, they have become reconciled and are disporting themselves even to this day. Then there was a rush of naked people fleeing for their lives, leaving thousands of pounds worth of heirlooms ground into the dust behind them.

" 'Mr. Martin walked deliberately to his hotel, nor was he ever questioned about the events of that night. Whether he married again, I don't know, but I know that when he died he left two grown, legitimate sons behind him, but whether they belonged to the first wife who fled from him, or to a second wife, I could not learn.' "

THE MARTINS OF BALLYNAHINCH

" 'Is Ballynahinch a grand place?' I asked Brian Mc-Namara one night,' said the old smuggler from Achill.

" 'Not at all,' he answered. 'When the first Martin, who was a trooper in Cromwell's army, invaded West Galway, there was no castle on the mainland, but Tigue na Builla O'Flaherty, the pirate, who lived in the Castle of Ard, near Carna, owned a castle which stood on a rock in Ballynahinch lake at the southern base of Benlethry. The walls of that castle are perfect to this day. Later on, when Dick Martin became chief ruler of the West, he used it as a prison, and any malefactor who was able to swim out of it got his liberty.

" 'When the first Martin conquered the place, a fine Abbey stood on the banks of a deep salt water basin into which the Ballynahinch river discharges its waters. This place is called Timbola, for it is here that old King Bola lies buried. In this fine Abbey there lived twenty-four Friars whom Martin took across the river to a little bluff or headland which juts out into the bay of Cloonisle, and he shot them all in the sight of their home. Since then, this bluff is called Curra na Brahir, or the headland of the Friars. Then Martin carried away the stones of the Abbey and built himself a castle with them on the mainland on the southern shore of the lake of Ballynahinch, an extensive, two-storey dwelling which enclosed a courtyard for drilling his murdering followers. Under this plain, low building there are many arches, and at each corner there stands a square tower, each of which has three levels. This castle stands in an old Irish wood, that is, a wood that was not planted by man; educated people call such a wood primeval, I think.

" 'When Dick Martin died, his son reigned in his stead, a plain, uninteresting squire who is only remembered for three things: castle building, going into debt, and getting an Act of Parliament passed, which was then called Martin's Act. It is much in evidence nowadays, and is called the Cruelty to Animals Act. This son turned the castle of his ancestors into stables and built a new one on a bluff which overhangs the lake, just where the river issues out of it on its way to the sea. This Castle is a long, plain, two-storey edifice, having no artistic design or architectural embellishment of any kind. It stands on the East corner of one of the largest moors in West Connacht, surrounded by wild Alpine country on every side. The son of Dick Martin had a craze for castle building. He built another one between Oughterard and the Corrib, which he presented to the Government as a military barracks.

" 'When he died, in 1846 or 1847, he left a vast estate to his only child and heiress, but this estate was encumbered by a debt of three hundred thousand pounds. The great famine set in, and there was no rent, so Miss Martin, who was then married to a Mr. Goubell, fled the country. She died in New York, a humble dressmaker. The peasantry of Connemara who adored her, called her Maria Martin. She was supposed to be the finest, most accomplished and most beautiful girl in Ireland. She always attracted praise, and when Daniel O'Connell stopped in

173

the castle the night before he held his great meeting in Clifden, he christened her the swan of Ballynahinch.

" 'This lovely girl went about accompanied by fifteen young peasant girls dressed in white, and as they walked along they conversed in the native language, for Maria Martin never spoke any language but Irish, save before strangers. Her name was kept fresh and green in the memory and on the tongues of the peasantry, but since these grand peasants have now passed away, her memory is now forgotten by those who have succeeded them. I have often talked to scores of returned emigrants who had visited with Maria Martin, and who had wept over her nameless grave in New York, and I have never talked to one whose dark grey Celtic eyes would not fill with tears as they described their sad pilgrimage. Alas, it was in her case the innocent fourth generation who suffered on account of the sins and crimes of the first generation.' "

HORRORS OF THE HALF-WAY HOUSE

George O'Malley, the grand old smuggler from Achill, was in fine form that evening as he looked around at the waiting company, and took another glass of pure barley punch from kind old Mrs. McGirr. "I have told you," he said, "that my friend, Brian McNamara, regaled me many an evening on my lugger on the Killary. One night he told me a tale which still haunts me on sleepless nights, and I will now tell it to you, but I pray that Saint Patrick himself will save you from the harm of recalling it when you are alone.

"This is the tale that Brian told. 'From Ballynahinch

Castle a vast moor stretches towards the South and West until it meets the wild Atlantic at Errismore, a distance of at least ten miles. It also stretches off towards the north-west from Timbola, at the head of Roundstone Bay, to Clifden, a distance of another ten miles. It is in the West corner of this vast moor that Marconi erected his wireless electric station, a truly wonderful invention. In 1798, and for long afterwards, there was no town either in Clifden or Roundstone, but two miles West of where Clifden now stands, as the traveller turns to Errismore, there stood a little Irish town or street called Ballinaboy, which consisted of about thirty low-walled, thatched cabins, fastened one to the other in a row. This town stood on the slope of a rugged hill, and had a bright, cheerful, southern aspect which commanded a grand view of the Alpine scenery of the picturesque region which stretched far away.

" 'It was a place of much importance in the days of our simple ancestors, for there were four fairs held there annually, and without doubt, this truly Celtic street was for many generations the home of the Muses and of the gods of pleasure. It was the happy hunting ground of all the strange peddlers, pipers, fiddlers, hedge school masters, and quack doctors on earth. I believe they never slept by day or night, and nothing was heard there save the wild notes of the bagpipes, or the loud-toned voice of the Celtic singer; from one end of the year to the other there was dancing and singing, as well as the drinking of poteen, which was then sold at five pence a pint. Not one stone remains now of that once gay place, and only the name of the townland is remembered.

" 'In those days all the packmen and strangers who

wanted to visit the vast region towards the South near Roundstone Bay, Cashel, and far-off Carna, would traverse the great moor before they reached their goal. In the centre of the moor there was a hillock on which there stood a house, nor was there any other house near it within a radius of five miles. This was Derryconly, the home of Anna More or Anna Connelly, who defeated the Claddagh fish wives in Dick Martin's election fight in Galway. Here she lived with her sister, Kathsha. In crossing the vast moor, this house was a land mark, for there was no road through the region in those days. In winter time, of course, many peddlers and others asked for lodging in this house, where they were received cheerfully.

" 'But any person who ever entered that house never left it alive, for the inhabitants murdered them at midnight. None saw the visitors coming, so there were no neighbours to criticize or question as to when they left in the morning, so the blackguards inside that house could murder with impunity. This terrible havoc continued until the inhabitants of that house of horror were far advanced in years. One evening, a peddler asked for lodgings, and was, as usual, cheerfully received. He seemed to be wealthy, so they murdered him and found that he had a large sum in gold and silver. In dividing the money they quarrelled, and the two sisters and a brother named Columb (called More-na-Irka, big Columb with the horn, for he had a lump on his scalp as large as an inflated bladder) killed another brother, the arch murderer, Breen Dharag. Then they bound his corpse with straw ropes to which they attached heavy stones, and cast it into the lake, which lay just beside the gable.

" 'The following summer, when the lake's level was

lowered in hot weather, some little boys and girls were tending cattle when they saw something white at the lake's margin. They imagined it might be a large fish or a dead swan, so with the inquisitiveness of youth they went to investigate, and were horrified to see it was the corpse of a man. They hurried home to tell their parents, who went to Mr. Martin. Yeomen were sent out, and they were greatly astonished to find the corpse was that of Breen, the red murderer; they arrested big Anna, Kathsha and Columb, who were taken to Galway, where they were hanged some time later.

" 'The house stands there still, and is used as a herd's house. A fine road now runs beside it, connecting Clifden with Roundstone, and this house goes by the name of the half-way house, for it stands midway between the two towns. For six long years I have passed that terrible house once a week, in all kinds of weather, and home by it in the evening, a journey of fifty miles, and I never passed it but I thought of Anna More or Anna Connelly, her sister Kathsha, her brother Breen Dharag, and the other arch-fiend, Columb More-na-Irka, and the murderous deeds they committed there.' "

A JOURNEY THROUGH THE WILDS OF CONNEMARA

"One evening," said the smuggler from Achill, "I turned to Brian McNamara and said, 'Brian, when first we met you said you had just come from a wild region which was far towards the South of Connemara, inhabited by a race of giants; were you serious or jesting on that occasion?' "

" 'I was quite serious,' he replied.

" 'Please tell me about that wild country and its inhabitants,' I asked.

" 'Oh, yes, certainly I shall, but you will scarcely believe me because the story will resemble Gulliver's travels,' he replied. 'That region which I speak of is inhabited by two distinct races of mortals, one a dark, small race, and the other a fair-haired race of enormous stature; even up to this date there is scarcely any intercourse between them. The southern portion of the Barony of Ballynahinch is a mountainous peninsula, thrust out into the southern Atlantic, and it is almost an island.

" 'It is bounded on the West by the Bay of Roundstone and the great salt water lough called Berter Boy Bay, one of Ireland's greatest, most secure, and most frequented havens for ships when Galway and Limerick carried on a great commerce with Continental nations in the old times. On the East it is bounded by the deep, picturesque bay of Kilkieran; on the North it is joined to the rest of Ireland by a narrow isthmus which extends from the head of Cashel Bay, in the West, to Inver at the head of Kilkieran Bay in the East, a distance of some four miles.

" 'This isthmus is a morass and is considered one of the softest and most dangerous in Connacht, so dangerous that it brings woe to the unwary stranger who would attempt to pass over it without a guide. This wild peninsula, until the introduction of roads, was completely shut out from all communication with the rest of Ireland on the land side; in fact, it could be called the Tibet of Ireland. It was inaccessible from the land side, but the natives carried on a great traffic with Lower Thomond or the County Clare in turf and black seaweed by hookers, and so it was quite accessible to refugees from Munster who came there, and very undesirable aliens they were, too, for they brought with them in their train the secret society, Terryaltisnr, which almost ruined the simple peasantry.

" 'Since the creation down to the time of the great famine of 1846, there was never a word of English spoken here, nor in fact until much later. When I visited this wild peninsula at the time of the Crimean War, there were only about a dozen persons among a population of 3,000 who could reply to me in English. And, although these people were Catholics, they retained all the manners and the customs of their pagan ancestors, and all their superstitions.

" 'They believed firmly, and most of them believe it still, that none ever died here save the very aged, but that all the fully grown, all the youths and maidens, all the infants and children who die here are surely carried away by the good people or fairies. In fact, until the introduction of schools and roads, which are of recent date, they were as primitive as the Firbolgs or the De Dananns, who fought at Moytirra in Partry some 2700 years ago. Their chief joy consisted in drinking their native Iska Baha or water of life, dancing and singing, for surely they excelled any other people in Ireland as singers of Irish love songs, for they were a very amorous people, may God forgive them.

" 'When I set out on my travels towards the South, it was in the early days of June, the most glorious month of the year, and Nature seemed to be prepared to meet the eyes of a great connoisseur of all her works. The great mountains wore their newest garments, the trees had washed their foliage which sparkled with bright dew-drops, the mountain streams were stilled, but as I approached them, they began to run and prattle. In the midst of the heath bells the busy bees were humming, and the little birds were twittering in the brambles.

" 'When I had left the Killary some six miles behind me, I beheld Lough Inagh with its numerous, wooded islands, and its strands of golden sands which sparkled in the sunshine, with the majestic Ben Bawn towering high above its western shore, while the Maam Turk mountains guarded the eastern shore. There they stood majestically like two giant sentinels guarding their darling lake, their magic mirror in which they had contemplated their rugged outlines since the time of creation.

" 'It was a sight of surpassing grandeur, but I hurried on through the deserted village of Finisglin and the ever-green Cloon-na-Karthin or the oasis of the forge, and some three miles further on I cleared the gorge of Glaninagh and beheld a sight I have never since forgotten, for I was standing on the northern bank of a vast lake which glittered beneath the rays of the summer sun. As I gazed down upon it with astonishment and delight, I imagined that I had accidentally discovered the lost paradise of our unfortunate first parents. There it lay in solitude and silence, well-sheltered from the cutting winds of North and East by the great mountains, while on the other sides its gently sloping banks were embellished by wild woods in which the Rowan tree and the evergreen holly predominated, and from which the cuckoo's sweet call resounded.

" 'Now,' I cried in ecstasy, 'I am surely the greatest man in Europe, for although I am an explorer for only half a day, I have discovered the long lost, much sought for Garden of Eden, and I have placed Humbolt, Mungo Parke, Livingstone and Stanley in the shade for ever. Marconi will look insignificant in the future when standing beside me.' Then I set down the date of my great discovery, and in order to make sure of identifying the location in the future, I began to map it out accurately. But, in looking towards the southwestern bank, I beheld something which nearly killed me, for I beheld a great village where I had thought all was wild territory. 'Ah, no!' I said, 'it is only a mirage.' I took off my glasses and wiped them carefully, then replaced them. Alas, it was not an optical illusion, but a palpable fact.

" 'There was the barking of dogs, the crowing of cocks, the neighing of horses, the lowing of kine, the bleating of sheep mingled with the milkmaid's song and the joyous laughter of children at play wafted towards me by the gentle wind across the placid waters. Then I knew that I had been forestalled by some other discoverer, and the shock was so terrific that I fell back on the heather and swooned away. Some years later, a gentleman named Sean Mahon, who I think was a Westport man, saw this charming spot, so he set to work and built a neat house on the southern shore of the lake, since time immemorial named Gorramon, but he called his place Glendalough, for there were two lakes there.

" 'Later, another gentleman named Hudsar passed this way. Charmed by the scenery, he built in 1844 a plain, one storey cottage on a little platform on the northern side of the lake at the foot of Lissouter Hill, in which is located the great marble green quarry, one of the greatest in Europe, out of which has been taken many of the pillars which support and adorn the great new Cathedral of Westminster. This gentleman named his place Recess, but the name given to this spot since time immemorial was Shraugh Sallagh. It is on the site of this plain cottage that the present Railway Hotel now stands. Later, still another gentleman came along, a Mr. Meacreedy, and he also was charmed by the scenery, so he built a neat cottage with French windows on the eastern side of the lake. It was a raw, bleak spot in winter, but in summer it was grand beyond measure, for it commanded a full view of the whole lake and the sunset. When I recovered from my swoon, I arose and pulled myself together.

" 'With much vigour and energy I faced towards the West, but soon I was confronted by a deep, dark, sluggish river, all overgrown with white and yellow water lilies. This terrible spot, which connects Recess lake with Lough Derryclare was then known as Beal Dhu Kora, which means the mouth of the black causeway, although there was no causeway, but only huge, uneven, slippery stepping stones placed there by Nature. As I went to investigate this terrible trap, I was appalled at seeing in the centre of the river beside one of the stepping stones, a young man drowned there, and his coarse Kilmarnock or Tam-o-Shanter, lay floating on the water lilies beside him.

" 'He lay on his right side, kept afloat by a great back load of willow and hazel brambles bound to him by a rope across his arm and breast. His mouth was open, and his grey eyes were wide open and seemed to be glaring at me. Had he carried his load on one shoulder as they do in Mayo, this terrible fate would not have befallen him, for his arms would be free, but the custom of the dead young man's country is to leave the 'crish' or hanger so long that they can insert the head in it; then the hanger is pulled down across the arms and breast, and so if a man slips, he generally strangles. I have in my time seen many deaths brought about in this way. On the opposite bank of the river, there sat a great, blue-coloured Irish wolf-dog, whining and looking at me with his great, brown, human-looking eyes as if beseeching me to rescue his master, but this was out of my power. I set my teeth and cleared the body with a spring, and then I drew a long breath which was almost a sigh, as men do who have escaped death by the skin of the teeth.

" 'There was no use in loitering, so I held on my course along the western shore of the lake, and when I climbed the bank I beheld another oval shaped body of water; when I thought that I had reached the end of this second lake, I found to my dismay that it was joined to another one in the form of an hour-glass, or like the arithmetical figure eight. The narrow spot seemed to be shallow for I could see the granite pebbles shining on the bottom, so I sounded it with my stick as I waded through it and passed over.

" 'Then I climbed a steep, narrow ravine all overgrown by a hazel brushwood, and skirted a fine cascade which roared and tumbled into the lake below. Soon I found myself in a great limestone village in the midst of the wilderness surrounded by the grandest landscape. I asked myself, 'Am I in Mexico, or in Peru, in the capital of the Incas?' I was in neither, but I was in the very centre of the wild, great parish of Ballynahincha. I had arrived in the village of Gurramon, one of the grandest in Connacht.

" 'Soon I was standing at the door of John Thomas MacJoyce, who kept what was then called a carman's stage, and his son, Neddy John Thomas, as he was called, one of the finest young men I ever saw, came to salute me and welcome the homeless, footsore wanderer, the friendless Mayo exile. Neddy Joyce brought me in and introduced me to the middle-aged mother, the most matronly and the grandest peasant woman I ever saw, and to his sister, the most beautiful, brown haired, brown eyed girl I ever beheld. She was only the daughter of a peasant,

> 'Yet England's proud Queen
> Has less rank in her heart,
> And less grace in her mien.'

" 'The modest, pure peasant girl hastened to offer me refreshments. 'Now,' said the mother, 'the first beverage is the prerogative of this Irish matron. When the stranger arrived, I put down the skillet in order to make him a possit. It is now just ready, so when he partakes of it from the hands of the woman of the house, then it is your turn to regale him.' A possit was fresh new milk boiled up, and when almost at the point of boiling over, a wee drop of thick milk would be cast into it with much care and skill lest it would turn into whey or curds. This drink preceded all others. Alas! I fear this fine old custom is now done away with in Ireland, for surely Ireland is much changed.

" 'The village stood on a slighe which could not be called a road, for it was only a narrow, paved pathway which wound around the hills from Roundstone Bay to Galway. On the street or 'Kimeen' I counted at Mr. Joyce's door fifty-eight Irish carts laden with herrings on their way from Roundstone to Ballinrobe and the interior of Connacht. The village seemed to be one of the largest and wealthiest in the province. This was not to be wondered at, for it had unlimited pasturage in hills and moorland, and it seemed to be the happiest community on earth. As time went on, the great engineer, Mr. Nimmo, began to construct the new road from Galway to Clifden. When he reached the lake, he ran the new road along the northern shore by Recess. This changed away the traffic from the village, so that in three or four years there was no trace of it or its once happy, prosperous inhabitants. A thousand times since then I have passed by this once happy but now deserted spot, and I always ask myself how is it or why is it that a million such once-happy villages with their chaste, virtuous inhabitants have been obliterated in Ireland, as if by the four winds of heaven, or by the bright, flashing sword of some destroying angel, while the great towns with their sensual inhabitants are left prosperous.

" 'When I had partaken of the viands which were so lavishly set before me by the hospitable family, I set out refreshed and found myself on a high table land which was a vast moor stretching off westward towards Athree, Ballinafad, and Ballynahinch, and which swept gently South, while high above to the East rose the wild mountains of Lettershauna and Glantirkeen. After I had traversed this wild prairie, I entered through a gap between the hills the bright village of Glantirkeen surrounded on all sides, save the South, by heather-clad hills. The valley is sheltered from the western winds by the high, cone-shaped hill of Cashel, from whose base it slopes gently down to a fine lake with many wooded islands lying

185

along the foot of the mountain. The bright summer's sun shines in this sheltered valley in all its glory. There it lay, the fairy valley, uninhabited and neglected, but not for long.

" 'Although tourists were scarce in those days, and their visits like those of angels were few and far between, an Englishman saw this valley and became so charmed with it that he built a neat slated cottage there. This turned out to be fortunate for the natives. His name was Daniel Bowden Smith, a retired Governor of Bengal, who was passionately fond of fishing, and here he could enjoy it to his heart's content, for the lake at the foot of the valley abounded with salmon. He was also fond of sea-fishing, and he rented and fitted out for himself another neat cottage on Meenish Island, adjacent to Carna, where he became acquainted with the parish priest. The acquaintance ripened into friendship, and they became inseparable friends.

" 'Mr. Smith spent his time pleasantly going up and down between his two cottages which lay nine miles apart. Then the great famine of 1846 set in, and the peasantry all around began to starve for they dwelt far away from the great towns and cities. Then Daniel Bowden Smith, the Englishman, began to stir himself. He ordered boilers from Dublin, each capable of holding forty gallons of water, and set them up. Then he employed men and women to attend to them, boiling stirabout to feed the starving peasantry, and he hired a family named Kelly to serve it out. Day and night, the boiling was kept going for two and a half years, and Daniel Bowden Smith saved thousands from death.

" 'In 1849, some Connemara boatmen took down the

cholera from Galway where it was raging at that time. Mr. Smith took the plague on Meenish Island and died there. The man from whom he rented the cottage, and who was always his skipper, stuck to him during his illness, coffined and buried him in the Protestant cemetery in Roundstone, and the skipper escaped the plague unscathed. Then the house in the valley became a ruin, and some vandal took it away. That house should have been preserved forever as an everlasting memorial of one of the greatest Englishmen who ever figured in Irish history. Alas, nothing now remains of it but its foundations, nor is there anyone alive today in Ireland who remembers him save myself. Five years from the time he died, his name was obliterated from the minds and memories of the ungrateful people he rescued from a horrid death.

" 'When I was leaving the valley where Daniel Bowden Smith once ministered to a starving people, I heard a sound that shook the great hills, and which echoed through the mountains until it died away like distant thunder. Again it was repeated, and yet again. It was the sound of some enormous trumpet, and then I realized, God help me, that the last day, the crack of doom, had come and I was called across the Jordan. I stood there in a quandary and began to cogitate. I said to myself, 'I don't see why I should undertake a journey to Palestine when there seems to be no compulsion, nor do I see any disturbance or upheaval of nature. In all my life I have never been brought before a court of justice for any criminal offence. Why now should I voluntarily offer myself in order to undergo such an ordeal before the Court of Heaven, and perhaps to be convicted? No,' I said, 'I won't go unless I am propelled by some supernatural force.' So once more I turned my face to the South and proceeded on my way.

" 'When I mounted a hillock I beheld the sea with the evening sunbeams dancing on the bright waters of Roundstone Bay, some nine miles distant, and my heart rejoiced and was as glad as that of Xenophon and his ten thousand Greeks when they first beheld the sun in their retreat from Persia, or as that of Pizzaro and his followers when they beheld the Pacific from the summit of the Rocky Mountains. The peninsula I had come to explore came in view with the dark blue Isles of Aran far away on the rim of the ocean. There it lay before me, this strange region with its innumerable lakes, its soft moors of vast extent in which rugged hills stood up like cocks of hay in vast meadows, all flanked towards the South by a great, long, brown mountain on whose summit there was discernible a lofty Martello tower.

" 'As I approached the soft moor which separates the peninsula from the mainland, I was confronted by a dwarf, or rather a pigmy, the strangest looking mortal I have ever seen. He was about four feet high, and he wore a high Jerry felt hat; his double-breasted coat was of brown frieze, and the buttons on it were as large as a small saucer. That coat would fit Jack na Bauna on his largest day, and yet this wee man filled it, and it hung on him with grace and dignity.

" 'His vest was of the same frieze material and double-breasted, and from it there dangled a closed jack-knive of at least three pounds in weight. His little breeches were of corduroy and his short legs were encased in a capital pair of brown, boxcloth leggings. Under his arm he carried a common tin bugle as large as any churn dish

188

I ever saw. 'God save you, neighbour,' he said in Irish. 'You infernal little villain,' I said, 'was it you blew the three blasts?' 'Yes, astore, I blew three little shadeognes,' he said, 'in order to inform the people of the country and the adjacent islands that I have arrived among them.' 'Who or what are you?' I asked. 'Moorkuseen na Muck, from Bohermore in Galway, and I cut animals of all genders,' he said. I left him in disgust and turned away.

" 'I crossed over the soft moor safely and reached a great mountain which is considered one of the wildest and most precipitous in Connacht, and as I entered a narrow glen at the foot of the mountain I saw an unexpected sight, a granite glacier which slanted down from a cliff near the summit. Since the time of creation, every winter the great boulders falling down from the cliff have polished this inclined path as smooth as a mirror. It is eternally wet, so that any living thing that attempts to pass across it is swept down and crushed against the great boulders at the bottom.

" 'As I drew near this spot, I saw a dead man in the glen at the foot of the glacier. He lay on his stomach, and his eyebrows, lips and nose were worn away by the friction and speed of his descent, and the ribs of his left side were driven in by the force of the impact. Against a large boulder beside him lay a tailor's lap-board, and out of his coat pocket protruded a large, black bottle, corked but unbroken. Horrified, I fled away from the place, and hastened to seek a rude cabin where some kind peasant would offer me a tumbler of poteen to forget the memory of that swift, terrifying death. Such sights are graven in my memory as I recall that perilous journey through the wilds of Connemara.' "

"Well," said the old smuggler from Achill," in consequence of all the old legends that Brian McNamara was relating, and all the wild scenery he was describing, my head was almost turned upside down, so I cried out to him, 'Brian, dear, I must see some of these places before I leave dear old Ireland, for maybe I shall never return. Anyhow, I must surely see Lough Inagh, the Prince of Lugatheriv, his castle and his fair daughter.'

" 'You can see all these things,' he replied, 'but I fear you shall not see that lovely girl.'

" 'Why not, Brian?' I asked.

" 'Because,' said he, 'for the last three years she keeps to the castle in such a way that it would fail Don Quixote in his best days to be able to get a chance of kissing his hand to her.'

"When the Rapparee ceased speaking, he drained his glass, so I said to him, 'Brian, I will sail from here to-morrow, for this is a dangerous bay for a smuggling craft to be anchored in.' 'How is that?' he asked. 'Because there is no way of leaving it save by the channel I entered,' I replied. 'By gad, you are right; isn't it strange I never thought of it?' he said. 'Do leave then, George, and don't delay, for if a cutter came in you would be caught in a trap, but I regret that I cannot accompany you.' 'Why not?' I asked him. 'What is there to hinder you?'

" 'I must say farewell to a very dear friend before I leave Ireland,' he answered. 'And who is that?' 'Well,' he said, 'I was never any good at prevarication, consequently I will answer you truthfully. I must say farewell to Nula O'Flaherty, the fair daughter of the Prince of Lugatheriv, before I leave Ireland, for we love each other very dearly. If it costs me my life, I shall do it.

" 'For three long, weary years,' continued the outlaw, 'I have attended Mass each Sunday in the little chapel on the vast moor, in rain and in sunshine, in snow and in frost, in order just to see the back of her glorious regal head as she knelt in her pew before the altar, for it is seldom I beheld her beautiful face. Then I would leave the chapel and climb to my home among the great cliffs of Benlethry, quite contented and happy. Sometimes I cross the Killary and climb to the summit of the stupendous Mweelrea in order to have a fond look at my native barony, Clew Bay, and the blue hills of far distant Tyrawley, and then my mind is at ease for a little while. These are the safety valves which keep my heart from breaking,' he said with a sigh.

" 'Just a few days before I first met you,' he said, 'I set out in order to visit Colonel Firebal McNamara, who lives in Cratloe in the County of Clare, and he received me kindly, for he is a distant relative of mine. He offered to keep me for life, or at least until the present storm of hunting exiles and outlaws exhausts itself, but when I awoke on Saturday morning, I thought of the fair girl who would kneel at the altar rails in the little church. I thought of how she would miss me the next day, and of how I would miss her, so I sprang out of bed and set out for Ballyvaughan. There I went on board a Connemara hooker that landed me at Carna. From there I set out across the vast moors and rugged hills towards Killary, a distance of thirty miles. I did not taste any food until I went on board the lugger, but I had my reward, for the next day I saw her at Mass,' he said with a smile. 'If you permit me to accompany you, I will remain another day,' I said. 'All right, George,' he replied.

"Next morning we set out early, heading South. The summits of the great hills were hidden by a canopy of clouds, white and transparent, which melted away before the face of the sun, and the bare, damp granite of the mountains glittered like burnished silver. We soon came in sight of beautiful Lough Inagh where on the western bank there stood the dark castle of the redoubtable Prince of Lugatheriv. When we drew near it, quite unexpectedly we met the Prince himself descending the mountain carrying a young red deer in his arms. We exchanged salutations and he, with his wonted hospitality, invited us to partake of some refreshments, although we were strangers.

"When we entered the ground floor of the castle, his wife, whom we had seen at the station dinner at Roger Coyne's house, recognized and welcomed us. She was surrounded by at least half a dozen poor peasant girls, busily engaged at household domestic occupations. Some were carding and spinning wool of various dyes; some were engaged at the laborious work of making a heavy churning, while more sat at a stack in the corner engaged in the most laborious work of all, cleaning and thickening a large web of frieze and flannel, a substitute for a tuck mill. There they sat, kicking against one another like fury.

"The Prince then led us by a stone stairs to a chamber on the second storey which was, I am certain, the grandest apartment in all Ireland. The walls were upholstered with the skins of wild animals, and the floor was carpeted in a similar manner. Four windows, facing the four points of the heavens, were glazed not by glass but by a substance made of boiled bulls' horns, a transparent substance which filled the room with a brown, mellow light, giving it an Oriental appearance. It was a chamber in which a Calypso or a Circe would love to recline and display their immortal charms to the enamoured gaze of Ulysses with, I fear, fatal results. Just opposite the castle there stood in the lake a thickly wooded island in which the fair daughter had a summer house, or greenan, and the wild notes of her harp were wafted towards us across the still waters. Alas! that was the last time her white hands would ever touch the silver strings of that much-loved harp.

"We were pressed to take food, but we declined, so our hostess brought forth a great tankard of punch, but not of the ordinary kind. It consisted of boiled goats' milk, mixed with double distilled poteen, sweetened with honey, a beverage fit for the gods. The drinking vessels were finely polished bulls' horns, embellished with quaint, antique tracery, far more ancient than that of the Book of Kells. When we had partaken freely of this wonderful mixture, we departed.

"In crossing a deep ravine which ran down to the lake, we beheld with much pleasure the fair girl coming towards us with a great bouquet of white and yellow water lilies on her arm, and she looked so fresh and lovely that I thought she could not be a mortal being. When she drew near, smiling as she advanced, she placed the flowers on the grass, ran forward, and clasped her arms around the outlaw's neck. She drew down his head towards her and kissed him on the brow and then on the lips, while I stood looking on in bewilderment.

"Then she unclasped her arms and said, 'My own

darling Brian, it is three long and weary years since I kissed you last.'

" 'It seems to me almost a lifetime,' he replied. 'Nula, my love, I have come to say goodbye for a little while, as I wish to accompany George, the smuggler, on a voyage to Spain.'

" 'If you did, I would surely die, for it is the consciousness of your being somewhere near me which has upheld and sustained me up to this moment. My health is undermined by mental worry and suspense, Brian,' she said, while her lustrous eyes dilated, 'you have startled and forewarned me, so from this night forward, I shall forsake home and parents and follow you to the world's end. And now,' she cried, with a sob, 'I swear here, at the foot of my ancestral mountain, that dead or alive, alive or dead, I will sail with you on board the lugger.' Then she kissed him once more and took up her flowers.

"When she was some distance from where we stood looking after her, her strength seemed to fail her, and she fell forward on the heather. We hastened to her assistance, but all of our efforts to revive her proved fruitless; the young woman was dead, and her pure soul had fled to Heaven. There she lay in all her youth and beauty a lifeless corpse, and in his anguish and despair, Brian cried out, 'O Lord, Thou hast destroyed the noblest work of Thy hand.' Well might he have cried out in his bereavement:

> 'Oh, ever thus from childhood's hour,
> I've seen my fondest hopes decay,
> I never loved a tree or flower,
> But was the first to fade away;
> I never nursed a gay gazelle,

To glad me with its fond dark eye,
But when it came to know me well,
And love me, it was sure to die.'

"Although the outlaw's heart was broken, he somehow pulled himself together, for he realized our dangerous position. He said, 'Keep cool and collected, for if the girl's father thinks that we, or at least I, had any hand in bringing about the girl's death, our blood will soon stain the heather. Stand off on that hillock while I go to inform her parents.' He went on to the castle and informed the parents that while we were going through the glen we found the young woman in a swoon or else dead, we could not say, because we were loathe to touch her. Their astonishment and grief were something terrible to witness. On examination, the father pronounced her dead, so he took her in his arms and carried her to the castle, while the great hills reverberated with the cries and lamentations.

"The wake was truly a Celtic one, carried out in every detail according to the orthodox rules and customs of the country, and her funeral to Salruck was one of the largest ever seen wending its way to that wild, romantic spot. While they were opening the grave, I was much interested in looking at the Alpine scenery which is unsurpassed by any other in Ireland, so I quite forgot the outlaw. When the grave was closed, and all was over, the outlaw was gone, nor was there any trace of him, although I sought for him everywhere until the shades of evening were descending. It flashed into my mind that he must have cast himself into the little bay and put an end to his existence. More dead than alive, I wended my lonely way to the ship and went on board.

"When the crew were piped down for the night, I began to pace the deck in great mental agony about the fate of my unfortunate friend, whose forlorn condition was a pathetically sad one. It is a terribly weird thing to be anchored alone in the Killary at night time, for the narrow bay seems to contract itself while the great mountains which enclose it on all sides seem to draw near. Being much worried and sleepless, that night my mental faculties became somewhat confused. I imagined I was anchored on a lake at the bottom of some enormous volcano whose crater gaped three thousand feet above me, and to make my predicament even more impossible, there was no egress from this lake. I sat down by the rudder and began to wipe the perspiration from my throbbing brow. Suddenly there was a slight sound borne by the night air, and as I listened I heard it again.

"It was the sound of oars dipping in the water, followed by the familiar rattle of the rollocks. The sound grew louder, and soon I saw a boat approaching. In the bow sat a man pulling vigorously on the oars, and on the stern sheets there was a coffin; my hair stood on end, for I imagined it was Charon ferrying some dead monarch across the dark waters of the Styx. Falteringly I cried out, 'In the name of God, who are you?' The response came back, 'Brian, the Rapparee.'

"With a vigorous back stroke, he ran his skiff beside the lugger. 'What is that on the stern sheet?' I asked. 'It is the coffin and the corpse of my wife,' he responded, 'for we were married three years ago in the great cave of Benlethry by the Augustinian Friar, Father Myles Prendergast, once of the Abbey of Murrisk. When she came to thank me for saving her life, Nula insisted that we should get married and await better times; so we parted at the mouth of the cave. Nor had we an opportunity of speaking again until the day she died.'

"All this was surely a revelation to me. 'What do you intend doing now with the remains?' I asked. 'I expect you will take it on board for a few hours,' he said. 'Why should we do that, Brian?' I asked. 'On your way to-morrow you could land us at High Island, midway between Boffin and Slyne Head,' he replied. 'In that island there are many hermits' cells. I shall bury her in one of them, and I shall live and die there, for I killed her, and I am determined to atone for it.'

" 'How will you be able to support yourself?' I asked. 'I have my gun,' he answered. 'The island abounds in rabbits, wild geese, and all kinds of sea-fowl which I shall shoot, for I never fired at any living thing that I did not kill. From the rocks all kinds of fish can be caught, and I am a capital deep sea fisherman. Sure, if I do starve, I have none to mourn or regret me.'

" 'What do you intend doing with the corpse if I do not take it on board?' I asked. " 'I will row down the bay; then I will place the coffin on the gunwale and lash myself to it with the mooring rope, and shove it overboard so that we will sink together,' he answered.

"I saw the man was mad, and would do just as he said, so I took the coffin aboard and placed it in a slanting position against a bulkhead in the hold of the vessel. Then Brian took a marline spike and started prying the lid off the coffin. He folded back the shroud, and there she stood before us dressed in the same cream-coloured dress she wore on the night of the station dinner, nor was there any sign of decomposition about her lovely face.

"Brian sat down on a sea chest, nor could all my persuasions induce him to leave off looking at her. Next morning I set sail, with the wind from the south-east. When I reached the open sea there was a great ground swell, and the waves were thundering against the wild headland of Renvyle. My heart sank within me, for well I knew I could not touch the High Island, which was almost inaccessible even in the finest weather, and yet I longed to be rid of the mad outlaw and his grim burden. We had Boffin on our lee, and the white spray rose and raved and dashed against the ruined fortress on its most southerly point, once the stronghold of the Duke of Lorainne; on those ramparts I had often stood and pondered in former days.

"When we came in sight of High Island with its great crag standing on the brow of its western cliff, the most picturesque object is this, I thought, that the eye looks upon on the road leading to Cleggan from Claddaghduff. There it stands, its spires and pinnacles silhouetted against the dark western horizon like the towers and steeples of the Kremlin in Moscow. When we drew closer, the island was enshrouded in fog, and the great waves foamed and roared all around it. I went below and told the outlaw there was no hope of landing there.

" 'Well,' he said, 'try to land me in St. MacDara's, or on one of the Brannock islands west of Aran.' When I rounded Slyna Head I had to take in sail, as from this point we encountered a head wind, for the coast line runs from here due East to Galway, some sixty miles distant. When I hove to in order to take in sail, a round hill of sea arose beneath us, raising us on its crest some fifty feet; then it fell away so suddenly that the craft plunged helplessly down with a crash, and I thought my day had come. Luckily, we had her under way before we reached another such wave, so she lay off towards the southwest on the tack out to sea.

"I went below then to see how it fared with the Rapparee. The coffin lay flat on the sheeting, and I was amazed to see the Rapparee on his knees with the corpse in a sitting position and his arm around her. 'Oh, great Lord,' I said, 'Brian, why have you disturbed the dead?' 'Quick,' he shouted, 'get me some brandy, for she is coming to life!'

"When I returned with the brandy, she was yawning feebly, so when she opened her mouth I administered about a quarter glass carefully. She gave a stronger yawn, and I found myself doing the same. Then her body shook; her eyelids began to quiver, and soon she opened those magnificent eyes, looked around her, and said, 'In the name of God, where am I?'

" 'You are on board the lugger and in the arms of your husband,' answered the outlaw. She was quite conscious now, and said jestingly, 'Now didn't I swear I would sail with you on the lugger.' We took her to the cabin where she partook of some refreshment.

" 'Cheer up, Nula,' I said, 'for in two or three hours I will land you in Cloonisle at the head of Roundstone Bay, within some four miles of your father's castle.' She shook her head and replied, 'Never will I return there. This is the third time Brian has saved my life, so we will go with you to Spain, and we may find some means of going from there to Jamaica.'

"At that time there was no emigration from the West to the States, so any person who emigrated went to

Jamaica, because some generations before many thousands of the peasantry of the West were transported to Jamaica by the inhuman Cromwell, and those who left Ireland later for Jamaica thought they would meet some of the descendants of their relatives on that island, but as far as tradition goes, I never heard that they did meet any of them. When the Rapparee and his wife refused to return to the mainland, I lay off towards the Blaskets. When we were windward off the Skiards, a great brig bore down towards us, outward bound from Galway. I hove to and hailed her, for I had known the owner for many years. There were at this time three brothers who were sea captains in Galway whose name was Yorke. Each had a ship, and each acted as captain or skipper, and they generally traded with Jamaica.

"The brig swung around and shook out the wind and I boarded her, but I was greatly disappointed to find it was not Captain Yorke who was in charge of her, but a young Galway man named Hart, whom I also knew. He informed me that Captain Yorke was suddenly taken ill, and as the ship was chartered to sail the next morning, Yorke employed Hart to run this trip for him. I told Hart the sad story of the Rapparee and his fair young bride. 'If they are determined to go to Jamaica,' he said, 'I will take them there with pleasure.'

"I returned to the lugger and told the couple that Captain Hart was willing to take them to Jamaica, and they were overjoyed. I offered the Rapparee twenty pounds. 'Take it,' I said, 'and whenever you feel able to pay me back, you can return it to me.' 'Oh, no,' he answered. 'When I fled to Connemara, my friends sold whatever means I possessed and sent the money to me;

so I don't need it, but I thank you all the same.' Then they went on board; the great ship bore around and her sails filled out before the wind, and she bore off towards the land of the setting sun, while I lay off towards the Blaskets.

"But," said the old smuggler, "from that day to this I never got tale or tidings of Brian McNamara or his fair young wife, Nula O'Flaherty. Years later I met a Captain Stone, a Galway man, in Flushing, and I asked him had he been to Jamaica since I last saw him. 'Often,' he said. I asked him did he ever meet or hear anything about the Rapparee. 'No,' he said, 'how could I when I never knew him at all?'

" 'However,' he continued, 'I can tell you about Johnny Hart and what he did to Captain Yorke's ship. When Hart took in a cargo of wine, rum, brandy and tobacco, he set sail from Jamaica, but not for Ireland. Instead, he bore off for Cape Horn, which he successfully rounded; then he ran down the Pacific, and never lowered a sail until he dried Captain Yorke's ship at high water mark on the strand of the bay of San Francisco, where now stands the great city.

" 'He took out her masts and upset her; then he cut doors and windows in her sides and turned her into a grog ship where he began selling their beloved fire water to the red men and the settlers. Later on, gold was discovered by a settler who was making a millrace, and who instead found gold within four inches of the surface. The clay which the first invaders put to back up the rude bridges was found to be all gold, so that in fact millions of settlers soon gathered there. Gold was so plentiful that if a person brought a gallon of milk to the miners he would get the gallon full of gold dust in exchange for it.

" 'The wealthy miners soon began to build houses around the drinking saloon, the ship. In course of time, a great city sprang up around her, and this accounts for how low down near the water's edge the great city stands, for it is only from twelve to eighteen feet above sea level. And the strangest thing of all is that in the city, which was founded of robbing Captain Yorke of his ship, his grandson, Dr. Yorke, is now Vicar General. Surely the ways of Providence are strange and inscrutable.'

"I agreed with him on that," said the old smuggler with a wistful smile. "But I would give the world and all to know what ever happened to the last Rapparee of the West, the brave Brian McNamara, and his lovely bride, Nula O'Flaherty, the only daughter of the Prince of Lugatheriv."

THE MAN-HUNT

On my first visit to the peninsula where Carna is located, I encountered many dangers as I made my way through the wild, mountainous but always beautiful region. One evening, as the shades of night were closing around me, I reached a great, rugged hill all strewn with whinstone boulders. A narrow strip of moor ran along its base, which was bounded by a long, narrow lake. When I had traversed about half the length of the lake, I saw in the twilight some white object under a small hillock at the end of the lake.

I thought it was a sheep, as it seemed to be stirring, but

when I drew near it arose with a bound and stood before me on the path. It had the shape or outline of a human being of enormous stature, and was enveloped in a winding sheet which was all stained in patches as if by the decomposition of the corpse in the coffin, and although I could not see its face or hands, which were concealed, it was hideous to look at, as it began to prance in a zig-zag manner across the path from one side to the other.

My heart seemed about to burst and a cold thrill ran down my spine before my courage returned. I walked up to the demon, grasped my stick and struck it a terrible blow with my left hand across the right cheek and ear, or where they ought to have been, and it fell like a log to the ground. The winding sheet fell off and I saw a spent man who was almost naked, and he was bleeding from the ear and nose. He wore no shirt, and his thin, much-worn bauneen was pinned around his emaciated body with a long nail.

He had no trousers on, only thin, ragged drawers, and his long, spent shins and feet were naked. I was going to hit him a second time and dash out his brains, but, as I looked at him with his eyes closed, his mouth wide open, and his pale, bleeding face, I held my hand, for I was sure I had him finished. I then crossed the remainder of the moor and reached a long hill, overgrown with furze; from the summit I beheld Carna, the capital of the peninsula, standing on a granite rock some two hundred feet above the soft moors which surround it. It stood there in the twilight, impregnable and inaccessible to all mankind save a native, for the swamps abounded with blind, mossy pools, all overgrown with bulrushes and wild sedge, so that one false step would precipitate the unwary into eternity, for he would sink, never more to rise to the surface.

I determined to lie down in one of the many shady bowers formed by the sweet-smelling whins and await the dawn when, perhaps, some native would be going towards the village, and I could follow him. Just then an accidental encounter relieved me of the dilemma, for some twenty milch cows came down the mountain and made for the village through the swamps. I followed them and soon found myself in Carna, the most famous village of the Barony of Ballynahinch. This celebrated village consisted of three houses, including the parish priest's residence, but yet it held sway evermore as being the richest village in far Connacht, a reputation which it keeps to this day.

Troubled in my mind about the man against whom I had delivered what must surely have been a death blow, I went straight to the parish priest's house. His Reverence was sitting in the kitchen, eating some stirabout. When he had carefully scanned my face and appearance, he said abruptly, "Pray, who are you?" I said I came from West Mayo and told him of my travels. "You have received some shock. What is it?" he asked. "Father," I said, "I fear I have killed a man." "Oh, great Lord!" he exclaimed in astonishment. "Why did you kill him?"

"He posed as a ghost, and thought to frighten and un-nerve me, and then I dare say he intended to thrash me, but I struck him, and when the blow fell I found this was a man, not a demon as I thought at first."

"How did you come to know he was a mortal?" he asked. "Because when he fell, his disguise dropped away, and he was bleeding from the ear and nose," I answered.

"Where did this happen?" he inquired. "At the foot of a vast low hill along whose eastern shore there lies a long narrow lake about two miles from here," I said. When I mentioned the place, the priest's servant who was standing in the corner seemed much affrighted.

"Oh yes," answered the priest, "I know it well. For years that lake has been haunted by a ghost, a giant who rises out of the lake and thrashes all who pass that way. Some years ago he thrashed my predecessor who was on a midnight call, and almost murdered him. In consequence of all this the lake is called Lough Boltha na Skalonga. Now I shall investigate this matter, and find out who is the villain who for years has been committing these outrages. Come along, boys," he said to his servant and to several other men who had come in and were listening in the background.

"We wouldn't go with you to that lake tonight," they said, "if you gave us Cishlan, Ballynahinch, and Dick Martin's property." "Oh, yes, you shall go, for I will put Dutch courage into you," he said. "Go and bring me a jug of poteen," he said to his servant. When the men had quaffed the water of life they were then as brave as British soldiers at the time of the South African war, and they followed their master.

Nor were they long absent when they returned, bringing the wounded giant with them, and they locked him up in a barn. He belonged to a quiet family who lived near Roundstone Bay. When he grew up, he went beyond control and fled to the hills, his occupation being milking the neighbours' cows, outraging the females who were caring for them, and acting the ghost at night.

Next morning the priest sent for his friends who took

him away with them. Some three months afterwards he broke loose again. He swam Ard Bay and reached Meenish Island; he could swim like a fish, for the wild waves beat and dashed against the gable of the rude cabin in which he was born. When he reached the island, he outraged a respectable girl, and she returned home and told her relations and friends. She belonged to the fiercest, the strongest and most relentless clan in the peninsula. They rose to a man and followed the villain, and then I saw a strange, terrible sight, a man-hunt.

Surely it was the greatest marathon foot race of traditional Irish history, for they covered a circle of at least twenty-four miles through soft moors and rugged hills, before the quarry was taken. He wasn't an idiot, but a sane, wild, primitive man, who when he heard the uproar of the wild swarm who were coming after him, knew and realized that his last day on earth had come. He knew that before night his eyes would close here on earth, and would open in the Great Beyond. He knew that if he jumped into the Crater of Vesuvius, this clan would jump in after him.

It was a race for life. The fleeing man had scarcely any clothes, but he was inured to hardship. He had no spare flesh on his bones, but he was determined to give a good account of himself. When the pursuers drew near, he cast himself into the bay which separates the island from the mainland, and when he reached it he shook himself like a spaniel and bounded towards the distant hills with the spring of a reindeer.

He bounded off through Rusheenacolla, Crumpaun, Carna, on through Lettercashel, and the romantic Letterpibram; he ran through Glinan, Shanock, Doonal, and scudded on along the shore of the placid, unfrequented Lough-a-wee, and the narrow, silent vale of Cowlaun, but still his infuriated pursuers were yelling at his heels. Then he turned to the East along the northern base of the precipitous Cnueg Mourdaun. When he reached the sequestered village of Derinish he wheeled towards the South along the western shore of the picturesque bay of Kilkieran, but still the relentless, swarthy islanders were on his track.

Then he ran through the great moor towards the village of Loughconeera, and dashed in and swam a salt water creek. And well he might, for certain death was just behind him. Then he ran through the village of Kylesala, Crearagh More, and Rossdoogan, and through the neat, well-sheltered village of Kilkieran, but yet his terrible foes were roaring behind him as he fled. He went through Bouraghard and Ardmore, Calageenish and Rusheenacouagh, and those who were watching on the hill of Carna sent up a great shout when they saw him coming at Sheedowagh.

On he came, head in air, springing like a wild deer, but when he reached the creek and the island strand, some of the girl's friends captured him, nor did they ill-treat him. When the other pursuers arrived, or at least some of them, for many lay helpless and exhausted on the moors, they bound him with ropes. Then they put him on board a hooker and bore him off towards Cortag-a-Meela, which stands out in the sea of Moyle, some twenty miles from any land, a rock which so often sheltered the white swans, the children of Lir, during their cruel enchantment.

They tied a chain around the man's body and attached to the chain the great mooring stone of a herring net, and they sank him in a hundred fathoms of water, nor was there ever a question about this action any more than if it were a dog to whom this was done. Some weeks later, a young woman was missing, and she could not be found, although her friends searched and sought for her everywhere. It caused a sensation for a time, but the incident was soon forgotten, for every day had its own outrages and sensations in that lawless country.

This girl had given birth to an illegitimate child by a man named Cosgrave, but he seemed more troubled than any of her relations by her disappearance. There was some talk about the ghost-man having freed himself from his chain, abducting and running away with the girl, but most people thought this impossible.

Six months later, the girl's decomposed remains floated ashore at the very door of her father's rude dwelling, and her hands had been severed from the wrists by some sharp instrument. Nine of the Cosgrave clan were arrested on suspicion, and one of them became an informer. It developed that Cosgrave had sent word to the unfortunate, unsuspecting girl to meet him at a certain creek, where they would take a boat at night in order to proceed to Roundstone to be married.

The girl readily agreed and went with the Cosgraves in the boat. When midway between Moyrus and Roundstone, they threw her overboard. When she rose to the surface, she caught hold of the gunwale of the boat with both hands, which one of the villains cut off with a hatchet. Then they tied her with the mooring rope which was attached to a grapnel and sank her to the bottom of the bay, and yet, strange to say, her remains floated ashore. The chief culprit, Cosgrave, died in prison; the informer was set free, and the remaining seven scoundrels were transported for twenty years to Van Diemen's Land.

THE SECRET SOCIETY OF THE TERRYALTS

At one time, many years ago, the peninsula near Round-stone was infested and overrun by the Terryalts. They were a secret society like Whiteboys or Ribbon men, introduced to Connemara, or at least this portion of it, by refugees from Clare. They posed as patriots in Munster, while here their patriotism consisted in going about in broad daylight robbing and plundering the wealthy peasantry, and a vast number of the natives joined them. They attacked the homes of the well-off people, taking away money, bacon, crocks of butter and kegs of poteen.

On a certain day they surrounded the house of a very wealthy man named Green. He was a boat builder who had five fully-grown sons, all boat builders. The houses in those days had no windows, so Green and his five sons stood in the doorway, each armed with an adze. When the Terryalts thought to rush the door, which Green had thrown open, the Greens attacked them with their adzes. Some lost a hand, some a cheek, some a nose or an ear, besides various other wounds. The Terrys, as they were called, fled dismayed, carrying their wounded with them.

When the peasantry saw how ably Green repelled them, each family began to arm themselves, and the robbing activities of the Terryalts were ended forever. Then their captain, a black-haired, swarthy man of enormous stature, went privately to Tom Martin of Ballynahinch, and became an informer. He gave the names of eighty of his accomplices, whose names were sent off to Dublin Castle. They were all natives who thought the captain was their friend.

There was consternation in the peninsula. The spy thought his accomplices knew nothing about it, but in this the villain was mistaken. The Terryalts assembled in a graveyard and cast lots who would kill the spy, and of course some one drew the fatal lot. There was to be a fair held in Roundstone in a day or two, on June 29. The accomplices were to begin a mock battle among themselves, for they well knew the spy would interfere to make peace, and in the melee they intended to kill him.

Clever as the informer was, he was ignorant of all this, while all the peasantry of the region knew his last day was drawing near, for in every family there was a Terryalt. The long expected day arrived, and there was a vast gathering of the wildest men in Ireland in Roundstone on that day.

The battle began, amidst terrific noise and uproar. The spy rushed in, and in a moment he was hit with a long splinter of granite, which buried itself behind his ear, sinking far into his head. He fell down with a crash, stark dead, and in a twinkling there was not a trace of the crowd, nor was an inquiry ever made about the slaying.

The body lay on the street in Roundstone all that long summer's day, and when I looked at the dead villain with the long splinter driven deep into his brain, I thought of that other villain Connor McNessa, lying with the brain ball of his foe buried deep in his head.

THE VILLAGE OF CARNA

When I first visited Carna in Connemara, it was known as the richest village in that region, although there were only three houses there at the time. It was evermore the mistress of the Barony of Ballynahinch, and in all probability it will remain so, for its present citizens are among the wealthiest in the province. Thank God and Nature, our granite quarries are supposed to be the finest in Europe, and our mines and other minerals are inexhaustible. The two lay inhabitants who dwelt there when I arrived were very rich, indeed, one of them exceedingly so.

He had one hundred and one milch cows, eighty-two breed mares, and I well recollect that one May norning twenty-six of these mares had twenty-six filly foals. He had 550 heifers, for in that country they never reared a bullock until after the Crimean war. He had a couple of thousand sheep, and two thousand yellow, gold sovereigns sewed carefully away in his feather bed. Now, wasn't he a wealthy man?

I have seen some strange things in my time, but the strangest thing I have ever seen was this man twenty years afterwards without a cow, calf, sheep, or horse, nor a four-footed animal, nor a brass farthing of money. The only cause the natives would or could assign for his poverty was that he added length to his dwelling-house towards the West. "How on earth could that bring about his poverty?" I said to a native. "Oh, sure, there is an Irish proverb which says, 'He is stronger than God who puts length out of his house towards the West.' "

The other citizen was reputed to be worth two thousand pounds. He was married, but had no family, and his queen was supposed by the natives to be the heaviest woman on earth, for she was twenty-seven stone weight. He kept a public house, where he sold the wildest and strongest fire-water on earth, and yet the natives drank it like nectar. He often went across the great mountains and vast moors to Galway, some fifty miles distant, in order to buy this terrible stuff, and also to buy Clough Gorm or blue stain to put on it, for if it didn't scald the necks out of them the natives wouldn't be bothered with it.

The night before starting for Galway he always boiled a skillet of potatoes, which he packed a pair of socks with. He then pinned the mouths of baileens together and slung them across his shoulder, and these cold, boiled potatoes, without any relish was his lunch on his journey. When returning, he always slept in a cave formed by three enormous, granite rocks on the verge of a vast moor midway between Carna and Recess.

This unfortunate man also began to build a room towards the West. When it was side wall high, both he and his wife fell sick and were given over as practically dead. In great haste, then, they sent a trusty friend to old Mother Clifden, the witch. "The crime is a heinous one," she said, "for he blocked the path where the fairies sleep at night, and where they pass frequently. I see blood on one of the cornerstones; the woman will recover, but the husband must perish for his crime is beyond forgiveness."

The woman recovered; then she took possession of the sick man's money and sold all his stock. She knocked down the new wall, and she very quietly starved the husband in the corner where he lay. He died, alas, without a four-footed beast, nor a farthing of money. The widow married a policeman, and whatever she did to the first husband, the second one gave her twice as much, and thereby hangs another tale. Another man arose phoenix-like out of the ashes of these two men, and like them he was wealthy, aspiring and impudent. But, like them, he finished off his old age without a beast or a foot of land. Surely, there must be some terrible malediction hanging over that fatal stock.

The inhabitants of the peninsula were, I am certain, the wealthiest peasantry in Connacht, as far as stocks and boats went. Each family had at least twenty cows, ten or fifteen brood mares, and from three to five score heifers, with sheep in abundance, and the dowry of each peasant girl when getting married was twenty-one cows and a bull.

Each family owned a hooker, some two, while others had four of them, and thirteen or fourteen smaller ones for various purposes. In the spring, each family sent at least forty hooker loads of black seaweed to Ballyvaughan, Kinvara, and Cranmore, and they generally sold at three pounds per load. In May and June each family sent at least forty hooker loads of turf to the Isles of Aran and to the towns which I have named; they got fifty shillings per load for the turf.

The month of July they spent fishing gunnard, of which they caught and sold a great quantity. In August they went out of sight of land in search of the basking sunfish, those lazy monsters of the deep. During the season, each boat would harpoon from five to seven of these monsters, and the liver of each fish was worth thirty-five pounds. The harpoons of these stalwart, intrepid men are to be seen to this day behind the rafters in the homes of their diminutive descendants. In winter they made enormous sums on the herring fishing, for at times a hooker load was worth as much as sixty pounds. Alas! artificial manure, coal, and railways have played out all these industries. In 1845 there were five hundred and fifty hookers; in the present year (1911) there were only five hookers in all of this once wealthy peninsula.

There was no kind of pasture anywhere, for the soft fens and moors ran down to the water's edge, so the peasants kept their cattle on the numerous, adjacent hills all the year round, but in winter they hand-fed the cows twice a day. It was a grand, interesting sight to see those cows when the usual meal hour drew near. There they would stand on the terraces and plateaus perched high, gazing southwards towards the island and the villages along the shore, waiting expectantly for their owners, gazing as Jacob of old gazed wistfully towards Egypt awaiting the return of his sons with the long-expected, much-needed corn.

When the owners of the cows drew near, the animals would rush headlong down the precipitous declivity, lowing with joy, like a sallying party from an almost famished, beleagured city hastening to meet a convoy of friends laden with food for their relief. And when I saw this wild, headlong rush, it often brought to my memory that incident mentioned in Roman history, how when the greatest general of antiquity, Hannibal, was hemmed in by his enemies amid the ravines of the Italian mountains, he let down droves of wild oxen on Fabius and his Roman legions.

Now when I reached this far-famed village of Carna where, all unknown to me at that time, I was to marry, settle, rear my family, and eventually to have my bones interred, I inquired for and had pointed out to me the parish priest's house, which was a long, one-storey, thatched cottage with three chimneys. I understood he was a West Mayo man who was far-famed for his hospitality towards strangers. When I entered, His Reverence was seated in the kitchen talking to four or five men of various ages who seemed to be servants. He arose and began to scrutinize me very critically, and I also began to take his measure, for I had often heard of him, but had never before seen him.

He was middle-sized and middle-aged, with straight black hair tinged with grey, and he was just beginning to develop the worst load a man ever carried, namely, a paunch. His nose was long and inclined to turn up, and his brown eyes were large and lustrous. Trousers weren't worn then by clergymen, so his lower limbs were encased in knee-breeches and black broadcloth leggings. This was the priest who when a young man took the great ride from Tully to Leenane on Maura-nee-Ortha, and who was the best-known and most popular priest who ever figured in the Barony of Ballynahinch since the days of St. Mac Dara, and the most hospitable, considering the smallness of his revenues and resources. Although the savage peasantry whose spiritual wants he attended to were surely the wealthiest in Connacht, they scarcely gave him anything.

His Christmas collection never exceeded twenty-three pounds, while his Easter one never exceeded seventeen pounds, and sometimes fell to thirteen pounds.

"A man he was to all the country dear,
And passing rich on forty pounds a year."

Now this is one of the poorest parishes in Connacht, and yet the Christmas collection is generally over one hundred pounds, as is the Easter one. This may seem curious, but it is easily accounted for, because the people in the days when this was a wild region didn't trouble themselves about religious matters until the hour of death, but then, believe me, lukewarm as they had been all their lives, there was a great parade of messengers hastening across the soft moors and rugged hills, calling for the Soggarth to hurry or you won't catch him alive, Father, for the sick person wanted to make a clean breast of it before he crossed the Jordan.

In fact, the priest would have starved among these wealthy savages were it not that he owned a mountain farm of about four hundred acres, about sixty acres of which were arable, on which he reared ten or twelve cows, ten or twelve brood mares, about thirty heifers, and a hundred sheep. He also had a large tillage and pigs and poultry. Consequently, he was quite independent of them, and he needed to be.

When he began the confession stations, his servant took the vestment box on his back, and they set out across the great moors and steep hills to the most easterly village in the parish, a distance of twelve miles, for there were no roads in any portion of that wild peninsula. There he slept that night in one of the dark, rude cabins, and so on from village to village during the week, nor did he see his own house again until Saturday night. After three months of this kind of work, he had to do the same in the numerous islands off the wild shore. Imagine getting a midnight call to one of those far-away villages, or one of the storm-beaten islands, but yet it had to be done, for he had no curate until he got prematurely old and feeble.

The priest's house was like a home for the aged poor and the wandering outcast, for his door lay wide open to all in need.

> "His house was known to all the vagrant train;
> He chid their wanderings, but relieved their pain.
> The long-remembered beggar was his guest,
> Whose beard descending, swept his aged breast.
> The ruined spendthrift, now no longer proud,
> Claimed kindred there, and had his claim allowed,
> The broken soldier, kindly bade to stay,
> Sat by the fire and talked the night away,
> Wept o'er his wounds or tales of sorrow done,
> Shouldered his crutch and showed how fields
> were won."

Not many weeks ago, a distinguished priest was telling me that he was often called to attend a very respectable old woman who lived some four miles from Carna, and whenever he would arrive at her home, the first question she would ask him was, "How is the Ahir Emon?" She forgot all the good priests who have succeeded him, but she never forgot the old friend who is sleeping the sleep of the just in his neglected grave since the tenth of June, 1859, that is, something over half a century.

This was the grand and great Parish Priest of Carna, that Father O'Malley who was the son of Paddy O'Malley of Shraugh, near Louisburgh in County Mayo, the last packman of the West.